Not a Minute on the Day

Ethel Stirman

'A land fit for heroes' the politicians promised, but Britain, post First World War, was still struggling to find peace on the home front. Having fought and worked hard to save their country, many were no longer prepared to accept the growing divide between the haves and the have-nots.

Although Joe and Eva were born in the same colliery village, they grew up in different worlds. Now, they would have to face drastic changes if they were to make a life together. Already struggling to cope with changes in their everyday lives, they also had to deal with conflict and hardship during one of the bitterest political battles of the 1920s.

Celebrate the Past
Embrace the Future.
Best Wishes
Ethel Stirman xx

DEDICATION

For my beautiful granddaughter, Katie, the light of my life and the love in my heart, that she may always know her story.

FOREWORD

Being born and raised in Easington, a South East Durham colliery village, I grew up knowing a lot about mining life. My father was a miner and my husband a colliery electrician so I have experienced first-hand what life is like in a mining community: the good times and the bad; happy times and tragedy; prosperous times and political strife.

I often wondered how my grandfather came to be a miner; why anyone would choose this life. I knew that he and my grandmother moved here from a small colliery village to the West, but that my grandfather was a hawker, selling goods from a cart, and my grandmother was a teacher of some description.

Like many other people, I left it too late to ask those questions for which I now would love to have answers. Those that have the answers are long dead. This story, therefore, although bound about with truths, is, of necessity, one of fiction. Apart, perhaps, for Joe and Eva, my grandparents, the other characters are not drawn upon anyone living or dead. I have, however, tried to keep everything as authentic as possible.

For those of you, like me, who grew up in such communities I hope this book, and the two I intend to follow, will provide your children and your children's children with one answer to the question: who am I?

ACKNOWLEDGEMENTS

First and foremost, I would like to thank my husband John for being my mine of information. I also thank friends and fellow writers from Easington Writers' Group for their valued support, comments and criticisms.

Horden Heritage Centre for their invaluable archive of mining materials.

Beamish Museum.

National Mining Museum, Wakefield for giving me first-hand experience of going down a coal mine.

People Past and Present archive courtesy of Durham County Council.

Andrew Curtis, photographer, for his kind permission to use his photograph of Easington beach on the front cover.

CHAPTER ONE

Greenall's Grocers, purveyors of fine provisions, took pride of place in the centre of the High Street, sandwiched in between the haberdashery to the left and the chemist to the right. Above the door, it declared that Thomas Greenall was the proprietor of this proud establishment and as one of the town's most successful businessmen, he adopted the air befitting a pillar of society. Granted, Wain Hill was quite a small community, however, in Thomas's eyes it was better to be considered a big fish in a little pond rather than small fry in a larger ocean.

Eva, Thomas's daughter, from her vantage point outside the shop, stood back from the window admiring her handiwork. Through the glass, gleaming in the bright sunlight, stacks of canned goods were neatly arranged behind rows of various dried products such as sugar and flour, the epitome of perfect order. These, however, were not the focus of her scrutiny. Reflected in the window, she was observing a young man unloading fresh vegetables from his cart.

Joe Fishburn, muscles straining against his jacket as he lifted a sack of potatoes, cut a fine figure. Although his work clothes were shabby, they were clean and neatly patched and his colourful neckerchief added a brightness to the day. It was obvious his work kept him outdoors: tanned skin contrasting with hair streaked blond by the sun. A brilliant smile lit his face and his eyes danced, for he was well aware of Eva's ardent study of his reflection. Whistling merrily, he nodded to her as he carried his load into the shop.

Still seeming to be absorbed in the window display, Eva inspected her appearance. No dirty smudges adorned her cheeks; no stray curls had escaped as they were often prone to; her white apron was spotless. She made herself wait a moment or two more before she followed Joe into the shop. It was imperative that her father didn't realise how attracted she was to this young man. If he did, then there would surely follow a lengthy sermon on the impropriety of young girls' behaviour.

Meanwhile, Thomas Greenall was standing behind his counter: ramrod straight in his white collar and tie, waistcoat buttoned beneath his starched white apron. Moustache neatly trimmed, he looked over the top of the gold rimmed spectacles perched on the end of his nose to survey the young man in front of him.

"Now then, young Joseph what do you have for me today?"

"I've brought a sack of taties, Sir, first of the

season, and some bunches of mint to put with them. Then there's the usual carrots and turnips and a few early cabbages. And Ginny says to ask if you need any more duck eggs?"

"I'll take a dozen, if you please." If truth be told Thomas was quite partial to a duck egg softly boiled for breakfast himself. "How is that sister of yours, Joseph? I didn't see her in church on Sunday; I do hope she isn't under the weather."

"No, she's strong as an ox, is Ginny. Old Sally, the sow, was farrowing so she had her hands full of squealing piglets. I told her I could see to them but you know how she is with her animals."

Joe's head whipped round as the shop bell sounded behind him. Framed in the light from the door, neither man saw the blush creeping up Eva's face, but Eva was delighted to see the smile Joe flashed her. "Hello, Eva, nice to see you."

"Nice to see you too, Joe," Eva prayed her father wouldn't notice the tremor in her reply.

Casting her eyes downwards, Eva silently made her way round to the back of the counter. "I've finished the window display, Father. Do you want me to put these vegetables into the racks?"

"No, I'll see to those but you can go with Joe and

he'll give you some duck eggs; it will save him having to come back into the shop."

Eva followed Joe outside, neither daring to look at the other until they were safely away from her father's gaze.

"Will I see you after church on Sunday, Joe?"

"Of course, you will, Eva, but we really need to work out a way to see each other for longer than a few minutes after church while your Dad is occupied with the Vicar. I understand why your father doesn't think I'm good enough for you: I wouldn't think anyone was good enough for you if you were my daughter either, but tell me, are you ashamed of me?"

"Oh, Joe don't ever think that, I love you, but it might take a while to convince Father that we belong together. I'm going to have a talk with my brother, Roland, maybe he can help us. After all he manages to run around with half the eligible girls in the neighbourhood without Father ever getting a whiff of what he is up to. You'd better go before he comes looking for me. See you on Sunday."

Thomas eyed his daughter keenly. He had seen the look that had passed between Eva and the young man. Talking to Joseph seemed to have brought some roses to her cheeks. He was proud of his son,

Roland, but Eva was the apple of his eye and he saw it as his duty to care for and protect her. Even though Eva had found employment as a teacher's assistant at the local Infant's school, at 18 years old he still considered her little more than a child. He was not naive enough to think that she shared his views, however, and he knew how headstrong she could be. After all she had hardly finished school before she had put her hair up and it seemed to him that she had found a staunch ally in her mother. It would only be a matter of time before she no longer wanted to help him in the shop and he would have the expense of employing a Saturday girl. Joseph was a good, honest lad and he admired the strength of character of his sister, Ginny, but he wanted more for his youngest child.

CHAPTER TWO

By the time Joe got home it was already dark. Although he was ravenous, he knew that the horse and cart had to been seen to before he could sit down to his supper. It would be best if he got straight on with it, for if he so much as set foot inside the cottage, the smell of whatever his sister Ginny was preparing for their evening meal would make his hunger pangs unbearable.

He unhitched Samson from the cart and lead him into the stable. Jenny, the goat, immediately bleated a greeting and Samson whinnied in reply. Joe lifted a good handful of clean straw from the side of the stall and began to rub him down.

"Eh Samson, I wish there were some way me and Eva could really begin courting but I can't see the way clear to it coming to anything soon. Her father's dead set against me and I can't say I blame him 'cos what have I got to offer the likes of her. Anyroad, she's bound to get fed up of me; I'm thick where she is really brainy. Perhaps I should have listened to our Ginny and gone to school more and off rabbiting with the lads less."

Joe made sure the stable door was secured for the night, then crossed the yard to the cottage that he shared with his older sister, Ginny. The youngest of seven, Joe was the last lad left at home. His father had been killed in a gas explosion at the pit, and his mother too had been taken young, worn out from raising two girls and five boys on her own. Joe's sister, Ellen, had married a lad from Bolton, Jack Surtees, who was a miner. At first, they had lived in with his parents but had recently moved to one of the new coastal pits at Essingham because there they could get a colliery house. Two of his brothers, Fred and Stan, now lived further north in Newcastle working in the shipyards. The other two brothers, Harry and Ted, had signed up for the Navy, determined to see the world before they settled down.

Ginny was the eldest and it had fallen to her to stay home and look after her younger siblings and her failing mother after her father's death. It had been her idea to buy the cottage and small holding with the compensation her mother had received from the mine company. At least with such a large family the smallholding had ensured there was always enough food on the table. Now, at the age of forty-two, Ginny was resigned to being a spinster, although things might have been very different if Edwin had come back from France.

Who knew, once Joe finally left home, maybe she would still find someone to spend the rest of her life with; Joe certainly hoped so but he also hoped they didn't come with extra baggage in the form of a brood of children. Ginny, herself, was in no hurry to share her life with anyone, indeed she was quite looking forward to having no-one to worry about but her beloved animals.

The kitchen was cramped but cosy. Heavy velvet drapes pulled tight against the cold of the night. Heat radiated from the black leaded range, on one side of which, a huge cast iron pan held a bubbling broth. That was one good thing about running a small holding there was always something nourishing to put in the pot. On the other side of the range was a set pot, which was kept filled with water to be heated by the fire; this served the family's needs for hot water for washing and bathing.

Every Saturday night, while Ginny visited her friend, Vera, Joe would heave the tin bath off its hook on the yard wall, partly fill it with cold water from the scullery, before adding hot water from the set pot. It was one of his favourite times in the week: to luxuriate in the warmth of the soapy water, the fire burning brightly beside him. It was here he most often dreamed of being married to Eva. How could he ever hope to earn enough money to provide her with a comfortable home?

As soon as he opened the back door, Joe was greeted by the delicious aroma of his sister's cooking. As was often his habit, he went straight to the pot and lifted the lid to see what was for dinner. Amongst the steaming mess of vegetables, he could just make out a ham shank submerged beneath the dumplings floating on the top of the broth. Joe knew there would be freshly baked bread ready to soak up the gravy; he licked his lips in anticipation.

"Put the lid back on that pan, Joe! It'll be another ten minutes yet. Just enough time for you to get into that scullery for a quick wash."

Joe turned and smiled at his sister who was busy folding clothes as she took them from the pulley maid above her head. Where Joe was tall and lean, Ginny was short, barely five feet, and round as one of her delicious suet dumplings. The eldest of Joe's siblings, she had always had a soft spot for her youngest brother. Her chestnut hair, now seasoned with grey, was drawn back into a neat bun and over her dark dress, she wore a spotless, white pinny. Her hands, never still, folded the clothes swiftly, placing them into a wicker laundry basket which she then hefted onto her hip to carry into the front room to await ironing.

Joe once again marvelled how Ginny managed to maintain her rotund figure; she should be skinny as the rake she wielded so expertly in the garden, for she was never idle: the cottage was spotless, the vegetable patch cultivated and the animals well-tended. In the corner of the kitchen stood a small sewing machine with which she made all her own clothes, as well as Joe's shirts.

Ginny retrieved two deep bowls from the small dresser in the corner and placed them at either end of the table in the centre of the room. "What're you standing gawking at, Joe? Get in the back and have your wash, for you're not sitting at my table in your muck!"

Joe tucked himself into the tiny scullery, emptying water from an enamel jug into the bowl. Rubbing the carbolic soap between his huge hands, he worked up a good lather and proceeded to wash his face and neck. A rough towel hung in its usual place beside the stone sink and he dried himself vigorously, using his fingers to slick back his damp hair. Most days he would have stripped off his shirt for a more thorough wash but he didn't see the point when he'd be having a bath later.

"Don't forget to empty that bowl!"

Joe tipped the bowl's contents down the plughole; the water ran outside to be collected in the wooden barrel that stood under the scullery window. Nothing was ever wasted here.

By now Ginny had finished setting the table and was busy filling the bowls from the great pot. "What do you want to drink, our Joe? There's some beer ready if you'd like a drop."

"No thanks, Sis," Joe replied, "I'll just have my mug of tea as usual, ta."

Ginny picked up the large, brown teapot from the hearth, filled Joe's pint pot, then poured her own tea into a dainty porcelain teacup.

Joe inhaled the steam rising from his dinner. "Ahh Ginny, I dunno how you can make a feast from the meanest of ingredients but I'm truly thankful for it."

They ate in silence. Ginny watched her brother fondly. She was aware of his love for the grocer's daughter and her heart went out to him. She would not, could not be the one to hold them back, she thought. Although it had been hard managing since the death of her parents, it had also been her pleasure to watch her younger brothers and sister grow and make their own way in the world. Now it should be Joseph's turn. But she knew he could never marry while their only income came from the small holding. No, she must make him see that she would do fine without him. And she would, she reassured herself.

"Here, give me your dish before you have the

pattern off it. No doubt you'll have a little more."
Tenderly she took the bowl from him and moved to
the pot to refill it. "Did you see your lass today,
then?"

"Aye, we managed a word or two when I dropped
those taties off at her dad's shop. I must say though,
I don't like this feeling that we're going behind his
back. Ginny, I was thinking of taking a walk up to
Brampton Pit to see if they're setting on. What do
you think?"

Anguish gripped her heart at the thought of her
young brother working down in the bowels of the
earth; in such dark and dangerous tunnels; his
strong, vital body forced into cramped, wet misery
every day; his young, free spirit imprisoned by the
inhuman conditions. But what other future was
there for him around here? Times were hard and
there was little work for young men outside of the
mine.

Joe caught the look of concern on his sister's face
but, as is often the way, he misconstrued the
reasoning behind it. "Don't worry, Ginny, I'll still
be able to help out here, although I might not have
the time to take the cart out on the rounds
anymore."

Ginny smiled at her brother's ignorance. She knew
what he didn't: how one day in the pit would leave

him drained of energy, weary to the bone, so that all he wanted to do at the end of his shift would be to drag his feet homeward to his dinner and bed.

"Don't worry about me Joe, I can manage this place fine and it'll be nice to hear a few coins jingling in your pocket for a change, instead of you just filling them with holes. Now be a good lad and set the irons to heat for me while I clear the table. Your shirts won't iron themselves and I want to get over to Vera's before it gets too late; she wants some of my liniment for her Jim's back."

Joe grinned; the efficacy of Ginny's horse liniment was well known in the mining community but everyone would smell Jim coming from two miles away.

CHAPTER THREE

Bella stared over her daughter's shoulder at the reflection in the Cheval mirror standing in the corner of the bedroom. Eva had blossomed into a beautiful young lady: the slender flapper's dress exactly matched the cornflower blue of her shining eyes; her golden blonde hair, now cut into a chic bob, swung smoothly as she turned to face her mother.

"Oh Mam, thank you, thank you, thank you!" Eva flung her arms around her mother, hugging her tightly. She knew that without her mother's persuasion, her father would never have agreed to even letting his daughter attend the Church Social, never mind the stylish changes to her hair and clothes. Her father thought he was doing the right thing by his daughter: he only wanted to keep her safe, but he would have to let her grow up sometime.

"Just you go and have a good time, that will be thanks enough." Tears sprang to Bella's eyes: she loved her son fiercely but, having grown up in a house full of brothers, Eva was the daughter she had always craved. "You will be the prettiest girl there."

Eva blushed. "If I grow up to be half as pretty as

you, Mam, then I'll do nicely."

"Away with you! Now downstairs and show your father and your brother what a picture you are!"

After Eva had left the room, Bella turned back to study herself in the mirror. Her hair tied back in a neat chignon now showed threads of silver amongst the gold, but her face remained unlined and her trim figure belied her years. Shaking her head free of vain thoughts, she turned to follow her daughter downstairs.

Meanwhile, in the parlour, Thomas was standing with his back to the fire, holding forth. His son, Roland, looking decidedly nervous, constantly pushed his spectacles back onto the bridge of his nose.

"Don't forget, I hold you responsible for your sister, Roland. Make sure she conducts herself with decorum and that she doesn't mix with the wrong sort. And don't let her out of your sight!"

"Yes, Father," Roland replied, "but we are only going to the Church Social not the Locarno Ballroom, you know."

"Where makes no difference, lad, it's the who and the what that I worry about."

Eva chose that moment to burst into the room. Wow, Roland thought, what happened to my little sister? Thomas stood open mouthed, eyes bulging.

"Well, Father, will I do?"

Thomas cleared his throat, "Very nice, very nice indeed! Now remember what I told you. Roland will be there to take care of you. I expect you to behave yourself young lady." His gruff manner was fooling no-one: his eyes shone with pride.

Eva quickly reached up and pecked her father on the cheek. "Come on Roly, we'd better go before he changes his mind. Bye Mam, don't wait up!" and with a laugh, Eva took her brother's arm and headed for the door.

As Thomas began to splutter his objections, Bella took him by the arm and held him there. "Now Thomas don't go getting worked up, it's not good for your heart."

"She looks just like you did when I first saw you. That, too, was at a Church Social as I recall."

"Well, perhaps it would be as well not to dwell on what we got up to in our younger days, Tom. Or the way we ran rings around my father."

Thomas took his wife into his arms and began to waltz her around the room. "I still don't know why you chose me, you could have had your pick of any young man in the county. But you must admit we do make rather a good team."

"Oh Tom, I do love you," Bella laughed up into his eyes. "Don't think my father didn't try to dissuade me from pursuing you so brazenly, you know he did, but he had to admit defeat in the end." That is why he had set Thomas up in business all those years ago but she knew she didn't have to remind her husband of that. It was still a touchy subject although Tom had proved himself over and over again. No, she had no regrets and they remained devoted all these years later.

"Eva is a lot like me," she continued, "and that is why you need to give her some freedom, especially in her choice of friends. Now see if you can find something good to listen to on the radio and I'll make us a cup of tea."

Back in the cottage, Joe was just as diligent in his preparations. He had shooed Ginny off early to Vera's so that he could have his bath and complete his toiletries in peace. Lying in the warm water, he dreamed of dancing with Eva. Up until now they had only had snatched meetings to get to know each other. The monthly Church Social was the nearest thing the youth of Wain Hill got to a real dance.

Although it was closely chaperoned and there were certainly no alcoholic drinks allowed, it still filled the young people with excitement. Joe had heard that one of the new bands who played the latest, fashionable Charleston music had been engaged to play. Although he hoped there would still be time for some of the more old-fashioned waltzes and foxtrots that would give him the chance to take Eva into his arms.

He knew Eva would be accompanied by her older brother, Roly, but he also knew that Roly would be too busy chasing the prettiest local girls to interfere with them too much. Besides Roly owned himself beholden to Joe for defending him against Ted Taylor, the school bully, on more than one occasion in the playground. They had remained firm friends ever since.

Donning his best shirt, Joe took his suit from the wardrobe and sniffed it; he could only hope the walk down to the Church Hall would dispel the faint aroma of mothballs. Time for a final check in the small mirror above the stone sink in the scullery. His hazel eyes stared steadily back at him; no remaining tell-tale spots of blood from his shave; nothing stuck in his teeth to mar his smile. He dragged his comb through his thick curls, the same deep chestnut as his sister's. "Right then, here goes."

Closing the kitchen door behind him, no one bothered to lock their doors hereabouts, he set off at a brisk pace across the yard and down the lane, whistling merrily as he went. He wondered if Eva would already be there or maybe she wouldn't turn up. Only one way to find out.

The sight of Eva took Joe's breath away. She was standing by the drink's table with Roly; the cornflower blue of her new dress stood out against the drab garb of most other girls in the room, her beauty enhanced by the golden halo of hair framing her face. How could he ever hope to claim this vision as his own? He was just about to turn tail and run when Eva looked up and saw him standing in the doorway. Her eyes lit up as she swept across the hall to join him. "There you are, Joe, I thought you were never coming. Come and meet the others."

Joe was relieved to find one or two familiar faces amongst the group of young people standing with Roly. Taking in the wide trousers and striped blazers of the other men, he felt rather old fashioned and clumsy. He was grateful that Eva maintained her firm grip on his hand as she introduced him. "Everyone, this is Joe, my friend." At once he was met with a storm of handshakes and back slapping; everyone eager to talk to him so that within seconds he felt part of the gang. Roly appeared at his elbow with glasses of fruit punch for them both.

"Have you added your own special something, Roly?" Eva enquired.

"Not for you, Eva, do you want Dad to have a fit? Remember I'm the one who will get it in the neck if you don't behave yourself, so no funny stuff, if you please!" He gave Joe a meaningful stare.

"Don't worry, Roly, I won't take my eyes off her all night."

The band began to play a foxtrot. 'Cheek to Cheek' resounded around the hall and Joe led Eva onto the dance floor. At last he had her in his arms for all to see and they certainly seemed to be a match made in heaven. The chaperones standing in the corner nodded in their direction muttering. By morning everyone would know they were an item.

Eva was glad when the band stepped down for the interval: her new shoes were beginning to pinch a little. Joe got her another drink and they stepped outside to cool down. They joined the other couples to disappear into the darkness at the side of the Church Hall where a little intimacy would be hidden from prying eyes. The soft murmur of courting couples surrounded them and Eva nestled her head snugly into Joe's chest. Joe raised her chin and kissed her gently taking care not to crush her delicate lips. Eva's sigh of contentment gave him all the reassurance he needed.

"I'm going to see your father, Eva. I can't go on sneaking about the way we have been. Anyroad the village gossips will be into the shop as soon as it opens to report on tonight's goings on. But there's something I've got to sort out first."

"Okay, Joe, I'll warn Mam, I'm sure she'll soften him up a little for you."

The rest of the evening past in a blur. Joe laughed as loud as anyone at his attempts at The Charleston. When it came to home time, Roly, it seemed, had disappeared. He was last seen heading for the door with Deidre Watkins.

"Trust that brother of mine," Eva grumbled. "So much for promises!"

"It's okay, Eva, I'll make sure you get home safely." Joe was secretly pleased that they would have the chance to spend a little more time alone together. He held her hand until they were away from prying eyes and then slipped his arm around Eva's shoulder. Walking along in companionable silence, Eva imagined how it would be if they were married and lived together. Of course, Joe would have to ask her first. A chuckle escaped her lips.

"What's so funny?"

"Oh, nothing really, I was just remembering something."

Eva's home came in sight. Joe kissed her, a little more deeply, a little more longingly. "I'd better leave you here, but I'll watch until you're safely inside. Eva simply nodded, turned, and ran to her front door. Looking back, she gave one last wave then was gone.

Joe's mind was made up: Monday morning he would take himself up to Brampton Colliery and get set on. He knew it was a long shot but surely then Mr. Greenall would see that he would be able to look after his daughter. He strode towards home, hands in pockets, whistling "Cheek to Cheek"

CHAPTER FOUR

Joe lay in bed, one arm tucked behind his head, and watched the sun come up. Yesterday, after church, while Eva's father had been busy with his Church Warden's duties, he had told Eva of his plan to seek work at the pit.

"It's the only way I can see to get enough money to convince your dad that I can provide for you, Eva."

"But Joe, you'll suffocate down there; you're used to being out of doors not buried underground."

Joe grimaced as he recalled the way tears had sprung to Eva's eyes; it was true, he did not relish the prospect of working down the mine, but he would do anything if it meant they could be together. And it wouldn't be so bad: he'd get Sunday's off and at least he would have some money in his pocket. Perhaps they could take a trip out to Durham on the omnibus.

"Make the best of it," Ginny would say. No good lying abed all day, he'd get up, fettle the fire and begin the breakfast. Give his sister a treat.

Of course, Ginny was already up and about. She, too, had had a restless night, tossing and turning until she could lie no longer. Better to be up and doing. As Joe came down into the kitchen, she forced a smile. "Now, Joe, there's some bacon keeping warm in the oven; pour yourself some tea while I fry a couple of eggs to go with it. And then you can get out there and feed Samson and Benjamin, they'll be wanting their breakfast too."

Joe shook his head in disbelief. Ginny, he knew, was just as keyed up as he was but here she was acting like it was any other day. It did seem to quieten his nerves, however, and he made short work of his meal. He best look sharp for there was lots to do before he could take himself off to the colliery.

By seven thirty, Joe was on his way; it would take him a good half hour to walk the five miles to the mine. The town was beginning to come to life as he passed through: Ernie Burrell already had his milk cart out on the road; people would be wanting fresh milk for their breakfast. Leaving the town behind, Joe whistled as he strode between the hedgerows. Soon Brampton Colliery came in sight and he headed along the main street between the two up two down miner's houses, where women were already pegging out the Monday wash. An involuntary shudder shook him; this was the same mine that had taken his father's life fifteen years

ago. That black day their lives had changed forever.
Pausing outside the giant iron gates, he took a deep
breath before entering the pit yard.

Immediately, he was almost overwhelmed by the
noise: tubs being shunted down railway lines; huge
fans drawing air through the workings; the thud of
the forge hammer in the blacksmith's shop. Above
it all, men shouting to be heard as they scurried
about the yard like ants, each with a job to do: either
feeding supplies into the gaping mouth of the pit
shaft or emptying out the coal that it disgorged;
sending it on its way to fuel the fires of the world.
On every side men raised their hands in greeting as
he crossed the yard, heading for the colliery offices.

Thankfully, Joe closed the outside door behind him,
shutting out the din. He was standing in a short
corridor with several doors leading away to other
parts of the building. Ahead he could see a large
staircase and to his right, there was a window set
into the wall, above which was a sign saying
"Enquiries". He rapped twice on the glass and
waited. The young lady who responded seemed out
of place in this male dominated environment but she
smiled brightly before she said, "Yes, what can I do
for you?"

Fighting to keep his voice steady, Joe replied, "I've
come to ask if there's any jobs going, Miss. Can I

see the manager, please?"

The girl smothered a grin as she said, "Well, I don't think Mr. Hastings, The Colliery Manager, would bother himself with the likes of you, but if you wait there I'll tell Mr. Garside you're here." Then she closed the window smartly, leaving Joe to pace the corridor nervously.

After what seemed like an age, a man appeared at one of the other doors. He looked to be about fifty, Joe thought, and was quite smartly dressed in a three-piece suit and green tie. "You looking to be set on, lad?" Joe nodded. "Right, come in here and we'll see what you are made of!"

"Right, just a few particulars first. Name?"

"Joe Fishburn, Sir."

"And where do you live Joe?"

"I live with my sister, Ginny, in Wain Hill."

"Just a minute, son, are you Freddy Fishburn's lad?"

"Yes Sir. Did you know my father then?"

"Aye, lad, and a finer miner never walked this earth. Now let's see what job we can find for you."

After that it was easier for Joe. He told Mr. Garside

how he made his living on the small holding with Ginny and how good he was with horses. Mr. Garside thought he might be best suited to working with the pit ponies that were stabled down the mine.

"As a timber leader you'll be responsible for your pony and for getting all the gear to the men on the faces as well as leading the tubs of coal out to the shaft bottom. Eddy Dowling is the Horse Keeper, you'll meet him on your first shift down the pit. I'll get Bob Stirling in to show you round the surface and fix you up with everything you'll need. Can you start day shift in the morning?"

As he spoke, he led Joe back out to the corridor, stuck his head into the office across the way. "Annie, send a lad to fetch Bob Stirling, please, and ask him to show Joe around and get him sorted. He's starting work here tomorrow."

Joe was a bit dumbfounded. His answer had simply been taken for granted; he was at once jubilant and terrified. Once again he was left to pace the corridor while he waited for Bob, who turned out to be one of the strangest-looking men he had ever met: his back was twisted and one leg was permanently bent so that he walked with a pronounced limp. His left arm lay useless at his side. Bob went into the office, had a quick word with Ann, then looked Joe up and down with a shrewd eye. "Rite young'un let's be having you. You'll need to get yer number at the pay office so you can sort yer tokens for going underground. Then yee'll need to get fixed up with a lamp in the lamp cabin, for there's nee lights down the pit tha knows. Lastly, we'll go ower to the stores for your safety boots; divent worry ye won't have to pay for them today, they'll dock summat off ye wages each week til they're paid for."

All the while they had been marching across the pit yard and Joe thought, for someone so badly crippled, Bob couldn't half shift. As they went from place to place, Joe learned that Bob had been injured in the same explosion that had killed his own father. Since then he had worked on the surface; there was a job for everyone at the pit. Everywhere they went, when Bob introduced him as Freddy Fishburn's son, Joe was welcomed warmly so that by the time they had finished their rounds and Joe was well equipped to start work, he felt more positive about the next day.

Ginny had been thrilled with his success, congratulating him thoroughly. Although he couldn't help but notice the frown on her face when she thought he wasn't looking. They had sat down together for a meal of soup and fresh wholemeal bread. As Joe dunked his bread into the golden liquid, then expertly raised it to his mouth without slopping a drop, Ginny laughed when he admitted he had forgotten to ask what his wages would be.

"I'll be able to pay you something for my board, Ginny," Joe said proudly.

"You'll do nothing of the sort, Joseph Fishburn," she retorted. "The more you can save, the sooner I will get you out from under my feet."

That afternoon he waited along Church Street for Eva to leave work at the local Infant's School. He knew the Headmaster, Mr Bennett, frowned upon any of his female staff members having suitors turning up outside the school gates, but he could not wait to give Eva his news.

Joe watched intently as Eva came out of school with her charges, smiling as she guided them safely out of the gates. Outside stood a gaggle of mothers, who proceeded, in twos and threes to continue their conversations as they herded their progeny before them. Several children were left to wait in the yard for older brothers or sisters: Infant School children finishing fifteen minutes before the Juniors.

Eva disappeared back into school, then re-emerged five minutes later with her coat on, pinning her hat safely in place. She turned right, down Church Street, seeing Joe immediately but maintaining her pace until she drew alongside him. To anyone watching, it would seem their meeting was one of happenstance.

"Well, Joe, how did it go? Don't keep me in suspense!"

Joe grinned broadly, "I start tomorrow, Eva, I've to be there at seven on the dot."

"Oh." Now the deed was done, Eva didn't know whether to be happy or sad. "That's great news, Joe. I guess those bosses know a good worker when they see one. But I have some even better news."

"Out with it then!"

"You and Ginny are to come to tea on Sunday. Mam has been working her magic. She is going over to see Ginny this evening. I'm sure that between them, Dad doesn't stand a chance."

"Could this day get any better?" Joe thought as he whistled his way homeward.

CHAPTER FIVE

From her vantage point at the scullery window, Ginny watched her brother as he lifted the next two rows of early potatoes. His shirt hung on the railings, discarded as he warmed to his task. The sweat on his back glistened in the evening sun, outlining powerful muscles either side of his spine as he repeatedly thrust the fork deep into the soil, levering it back to unearth the crop. Stooping he stripped the golden globes from the roots and tossed them into a waiting wheelbarrow. Soon that back would be black as coal, she thought, scarred by the stark conditions down the pit; everyday he would face danger: roof falls, accidents, explosions …

Ginny's nose warned her the cakes in her oven were almost done. Giving the bottom of the pan a final scrub, she rinsed it then turned it over onto the wooden draining board to dry. Before too long Bella would arrive on her doorstep and she did not want to greet her in her working clothes with flour on her face and tats in her hair. She smiled at her own misplaced vanity.

"Joe! You'd best get in here and make yourself presentable. Bella will be here soon and you never know she might bring young Eva along with her."

Straightening up, Joe reached for his shirt, "Alright Sis, I'll be right there." Grinning, he pushed the laden barrow over to the stable and disgorged its contents into a low, wooden box. Later, he would sort the potatoes into hessian sacks ready to be loaded onto the cart for the week's rounds.

Ginny reached into the oven, protecting her hands with a kitchen towel, and lifted the tray of Queen cakes onto the hearth to cool. Even if she put on her best dress, she knew it would come nowhere near to the fine clothes Bella always wore. However, no matter the differences in their roots, Ginny liked and respected Bella. Hadn't she stood her ground against her father to marry Tom Greenall despite his humble origins? Yes, Bella had been a good wife to Tom and if anyone had ideas above their station, it was Tom not Bella who was guilty. But Ginny had known Tom a long time: they had grown up together on the same street. She also remembered how Tom and his mother, had suffered at the hands of his drunken brute of a father. If Tom was a bit overprotective of his daughter then it was quite understandable, just so long as he didn't try to say that her brother, Joe, was not good enough to become one of his family.

At last Ginny was tidied, the fruited Queen cakes arranged on her best plate and the kettle singing on the hob in front of the fire. Joe, too, had had a wash and changed his clothes. He kept walking to the open door to peer down the lane for any sign of the visitor.

"For goodness sake Joe, sit down. You'll wear a hole in the mat with your pacing."

Lowering himself onto one of the chairs beside the table, Joe at once began fiddling with the plate of cakes before him.

"Out! Out! Before I take the broom to you!"

"Sorry Ginny," said Joe, pushing the plate back into the middle of the table. "I wasn't this nervous when I met that boss feller at the pit this morning. Do you really think Eva will come with her Mam? She didn't say anything when I met her after school." Ginny almost felt sorry for him, the great soft fool.

Relief came with the sound of voices echoing down the lane. The excited babble of Eva's voice almost matching Joe's nervousness. Both knew there might be a lot depending on the outcome of this evening's meeting. Ginny rose from her chair to greet her visitors.

"Hello Bella, Eva, come along in and find a seat

while I make us a cup of tea. Joe take the ladies' jackets and put them in the front room."

Bella and Eva settled themselves at the table, flattered to realise that Ginny thought enough of them as friends not strangers to be shown into the front parlour.

Eva and Joe hardly dared look at each other, instead stealing furtive glances when they thought the women's attention was elsewhere. "Oh, for Heaven's sake," Bella at last exclaimed. "Why don't you young ones take yourselves off for a walk down the lane and leave Ginny and me in peace? We've got a lot to discuss." The young couple didn't need telling twice; they shot out of the kitchen door as if the hounds of hell were after them.

Ginny replenished their teacups and offered Bella the plate of cakes. "I really shouldn't," Bella hesitated, finally taking one of the Queen cakes, "but I don't get the chance to sample your delicious baking very often."

"Hmmm," Ginny mused, "I get the feeling that we will be seeing a lot more of you, Bella, and Eva in the future."

"Yes, well that is what I've come to talk with you about Ginny. I think we both know how Joe and

Eva feel about each other, and I, for one, am certainly in favour of the match. There isn't a kinder, more upstanding man in the area than your Joe; he's a credit to you. I know that no matter what he will always work hard to provide for Eva, and more importantly, he makes her very happy."

"Aye Bella he's a fine lad, right enough: he never gives me a moment's worry except for his future. We both know that he'll never make enough to keep a family working this small holding with me."

"But Eva tells me he's to start work at the mine tomorrow."

"That's what worries me most. I don't know how he'll cope with being trapped down that dark hole for eight hours a day, and then there's the reminder of what happened to his Dad. How do you live with that kind of fear every day?"

"Now Ginny it's no good getting yourself upset; the lad's made up his mind and anyway, Eva tells me he's to be working with the ponies, not at the coal face, so that will suit him down to the ground."

"Right," Ginny shrugged her shoulders, "that's enough of my worries, let's get down to the real reason you're here: Tom!"

"Just leave Tom to me; we both know his heart's in

the right place; he might grumble and bluster but he knows Joe's a fine lad and will make a good husband for Eva. That is why he's agreed that you and Joe should come over to tea on Sunday. If we are going to be a family it's time we started acting like one. Now what can you tell me about the new people who've moved into Casson Street? They come from somewhere down South, I hear."

Up on the hill overlooking the village, the young couple had made themselves comfortable on Joe's jacket, spread out over the grass. Joe chewed thoughtfully on a piece of grass while Eva picked cowslips which grew in abundance around them. Now that they at last had some time alone, neither knew quite what to say.

Below them Wain Hill dozed peacefully in the evening sunshine. Not much more than a church, a school and a street of shops surrounded by a few rows of miners' cottages: mean, two up, two down terraced houses, huddled together for economy rather than comfort, with sunless back yards housing an outdoor netty and a coal house. Married men could apply to live in one of these colliery houses; many held families of five or six or seven.

Several stood empty now; Wain Hill mine was almost worked out; only two seams remained in coal production where there had once been coal faces on four levels. Every day men lay on their sides in the narrow seams, digging out coal with pick axes while others shovelled it back to the waiting tubs; back- breaking work but at least it meant a pay at the end of the week. Many men had been laid off and once your employment at the pit ceased then so did your entitlement to free housing.

Brampton Colliery lay five miles to the north: a dark smudge on the landscape. Sunk much later than Wain Hill, it used more modern mining methods and still worked four seams. Many of the men who had been laid off from Wain Hill had transferred there and because the same company owned both pits they could remain in their tied housing. This suited their wives who had no wish to move away from the comfort and security of their extended families. A lot of these women had not even moved out of the street where they were born.

"Penny for them," Eva said quietly, bringing Joe out of his reverie.

"I was just thinking about tomorrow," Joe replied. "I'll be glad to get the first shift over with; at least then I'll know what to expect. It's the uncertainty that cripples your mind."

"I know. I keep trying to imagine what it must be like. I suppose it is a bit like being down our coal cellar but much bigger and probably much darker."

"They reckon it's so dark you can't see a hand in front of your face. But at least if all the men are as friendly as those I met today, they'll steer me clear 'til I find my feet. And I must admit I'm quite looking forward to meeting my pit pony and getting to know him."

Eva moved closer. "It's strange to think of there being stables down the mine, Joe. Those poor ponies working down there every minute of every day in the cold and the dark."

"Aye it must be a hard life for them but no harder than for a lot of horses up here. They only work one shift a day, same as the men, and at least they have a dry bed in their stalls and plenty of food. If the ponies weren't there to do a lot of the heavy pulling and shifting, it would be a lot harder on the miners. And, don't forget, they're brought to the surface to run free in the fields for two weeks every summer during the pit shut down when there's not enough men left in the mine to feed them."

The sun began to sink lower. Eva shivered as the evening grew colder. As they stood up to make their way back down to the cottage, Joe drew Eva to him, wrapping his rough jacket around her slender shoulders for warmth. Their kisses had become more passionate of late, but tonight there was only tenderness as they felt in that moment the importance of moving on. Tomorrow would be the first day of the rest of their lives together.

CHAPTER SIX

Cold drizzle soaked the land next morning as Joe strode down the lane, joining others on their way to Brampton. Dressed in his oldest shirt and trousers, a ragged jacket and flat cap kept out most of the wet. The new leather boots, making his footsteps heavy, completed his outfit. His only burden was a canvas shoulder bag holding his water bottle and bait: jam sandwiches and an apple. Ginny had been up before him, as usual, sorting his breakfast. She had assured him that something sweet would be most welcome down the pit.

Never before had he faced such uncertainty.

As they tramped through the streets of Brampton, so their numbers grew. Most of the men were silent, their mood matched by the weather, but one or two greeted him gruffly. Nearing the pit gates, the sounds of the yard rang out, calling them to work. They marched in unison towards the lamp cabin. Each man collected two tokens from the board, one triangular, one round, then joined the line to receive his miner's safety lamp from the lamp man. Every lamp had to be lit in the safety of the cabin; the ever-present danger of explosion foremost in their minds. Only the deputies were allowed to strike up a lamp down the pit. Without your lamp you were marooned in total blackness.

As they approached the cage that would carry them down the shaft to the seams below, Bob Stirling appeared at his elbow.

"You didn't change your mind then?" Bob quipped. "This here's Bill; he'll see you down and show you where the stables are. You're to report to Eddy Dowling, the Head Horsekeeper. Diven't worry, you'll be fine once ye've got yer fust shift ower."

Joe watched the little man limp off, then turned as Bill spoke to him, "I hear you're Freddy Fishburn's lad. Keep with me when we get into the cage and try to keep away from the edge. The speed'll likely give you a bit of a fright at first but ye'll soon get used to it."

As each man got into the cage, he was first patted down to ensure he wasn't carrying any contraband in the form of cigarettes or matches. Then he gave the Banksman his triangular token with his number stamped on it: these would be taken to the pay office to be recorded, then hung back on the board to show which men were down the pit. Joe placed the other round token into his pocket; he would need to give this to the Banksman at the end of his shift when he rode the cage back up. In this way no man could ever go missing underground.

The men were packed into the cage, pressed hard together like sardines in a tin. Bill told him to make sure to bend his knees slightly as the cage first did away as it gave quite a jolt when the brake was released. The chain gate rattled ominously trapping them inside, before the outer gate was slammed shut. Two signal raps rang out and their journey began.

Descending into the darkness, no-one spoke but Joe could hear and feel the air pressure building. His heart's rapid beating pounded in his ears as they hurtled down through the blackness. Soon the other cage in the shaft which counter balanced their own was nearing, then passing them, as they continued to plummet down. Suddenly light appeared below as they drew up to the Low Main seam. The cage jerked to a halt. The descent had only taken two or three minutes but had seemed a lifetime to Joe. It felt like descending into the bowels of the earth.

The hewers, fillers and putters hurried to their respective coal faces to meet up with the deputy at his kist; he would tell them what jobs they would be doing that shift. Many of these teams had worked together for years and this daily routine was as familiar to them as putting on a favourite cardigan. The pit community was a close one, above ground as well as below. Anyone who couldn't be completely trusted to have your back would soon find his marching orders waiting.

Joe copied Bill as he hooked his lamp onto his belt. "Right lad, follow me and keep close for we'll soon lose the light away from the shaft bottom."

They were in a dark tunnel, a roadway of sorts, hardly high enough to let a man stand so Joe had to take care not to catch his head on the overhead girders supporting the roof. If you stretched out your arms you could touch both sides. Joe fought the claustrophobia that was threatening to overcome him.

The floor was rough making walking difficult. Lamplight glinted off two steel rails that carried the tubs in and out of the workings. "Try to keep to the sleepers," Bill advised, "sometimes the floor falls away sharp and you'll find yersel down a hole if yer not careful." Joe shortened his step and instantly recognised the shuffling gait he had often seen amongst the older miners.

Walking through the darkness, he could hear the mine breathing around him. Circulating air brushed his face, as he listened to the sighings, creaks and cracks. Joe wondered if they were in imminent danger of being buried alive but Bill continued along the tunnel unconcerned. "Yer'll learn to listen to the pit, lad. She'll give you fair warning if she's about to come down. And always tak notice of your lamp, watch the flame cos if it starts to turn blue ye know there's gas about and ye'll need to get out smartish."

Bob Stirling had warned Joe about the dangers of methane gas down the mine. Mixed with the coal dust in the air it was highly explosive. It had been the cause of the devastating explosion that had taken his father and the other miners with him. Even worse, it was well named 'the silent death' because it was colourless and odourless and could suffocate you in minutes.

"Always hang your lamp high cos the gas is lighter than air so you'll get an early warning if it's about. Then tell the deputy to get the ventilation team in to clear it."

Joe shuddered. The mine smells were so alien to him: the cold, dank smell of coal dust seemed to clog his airways but it wasn't just the cold that caused him to shiver.

After five minutes steady walking they came out of the tunnel into the underground stables. It was little more than a large, square box hewn out of the stone and coal, with a row of six stalls on either side. On one side three of the stalls were empty and Joe could see that each stall had a feed trough, a bag of hay slung from a prop, a bucket of water and hooks to hold the horses' harness. At this end of the stable,

Eddy Dowling was supervising a young lad who was busy mucking out: raking out all the dirty, used bedding and replacing it with fresh, clean straw. "After yer've finished that, you can change the water and hay for fresh, and put some feed in the troughs. Not too many oats, mind, we don't need frisky ponies!"

Eddy turned and looked at Joe. "You'll be Joseph Fishburn, I suppose. They tell me yer good with horses." Joe simply nodded in reply. "Well, if yer half as good as they say yer'll be welcome here. I haven't really had someone with a feel for the beasts since Jimmy got hisself lamed." Walking over to the pony in the fourth stall, Eddy beckoned Joe nearer. "This is Benji. He's a fine lad but I dare say he's a bit smaller than the hosses yer used to. You'll learn to love him though cos he'll teach you more about the mine than the best miner ever could."

All the while Eddy was rubbing the back of the pony's ears, then stroking his velvety muzzle. "Yer'll look after him afore yersel. Mak sure he's washed and rubbed down at the end of every shift and if he's done well gie him the crusts off your bait. Let's see how you get on with putting his limbers on."

Eddy stayed with Joe for most of his shift; not for Joe's sake but to see that Benji was not mistreated. His wife always joked that if Eddy could've taken the ponies home with him, she would soon have been turfed out of their double bed.

Joe was to be responsible for bringing supplies up to the faces where needed and for taking full tubs back to the wayend at the shaft for loading into the cage, where they would then be raised to the surface or bank as it was known. Although Benji took the hard work out of ferrying materials down the long tunnels, Joe still had a lot of lifting to do and although he thought himself fit, he found himself tiring.

About halfway through his shift, Joe stopped to have his bait with some of the other timber leaders. Earlier he had discarded his jacket, leaving it, and his canvas bag, hanging on a prop near the outbye wagonway. One of the men advised him always to check the roof was sound above his head, and to sit on a piece of wood with his back to a prop. Safety always had to be uppermost in every miner's mind.

He reached into his bag and took out the jam sandwiches Ginny had made for him that morning. She had carefully wrapped them in waxed paper to keep them fresh. He could almost taste them already and licked his lips in anticipation. Imagine his horror when he found a hole drilled through the middle of his bait. The men around him let out great guffaws of laughter. "Looks like the mice got there afore ye," one of them laughed. "Now you know why we always keep our bait in a tin." Joe, however, was so hungry, he was determined not to be bested by a greedy rodent; he carefully ate his way around the hole, saving what was left as a treat for Benji later.

CHAPTER SEVEN

Breakfast had been an unusually quiet affair in the Greenall household. Eva, normally full of plans and chatter for the day ahead, had been remarkably silent. Thomas regarded her over his spectacles as he read his morning paper, watching her push her eggs aimlessly around her plate. Catching his wife's eye, he raised his eyebrows to question the strange behaviour of his daughter but Bella warned him off with a tiny shake of her head.

Giving up any pretence of hunger, Eva asked to be excused from the table. Bella reached over and patted her daughter's hand comfortingly, "Don't worry about Joe, I'm sure he'll be just fine." Although Eva gave her mother a brief smile, she couldn't help wishing the day was over.

Entering the staffroom that morning, Eva was grateful to be usefully occupied. As the most junior member of staff, it fell to her to fill the kettle and prepare cups and saucers for tea for the rest of the teachers as they came in.

Outside in the yard, the general hubbub of children's games filtered through the open window. Eva was relieved as the first to arrive was her friend and confidante, Lucy Grainger. Lucy had been in the year above Eva at school and had immediately befriended Eva, ensuring she was aware of the many rules and etiquettes her role as Junior Teacher entailed. Many of the more senior members of staff demanded much more respect than they could rightfully be said to deserve. Eva especially didn't like the free and easy way some of them meted out corporal punishment, usually with a wickedly cruel cane, for seemingly trivial misdemeanours.

"Good morning, Eva," Lucy breezed into the staffroom. "And how are you this miserable Tuesday?"

"I am probably feeling a bit better than Joe is right now," Eva replied glumly.

"By the look on your face I wouldn't bet on it. Talk about lost a shilling and found a penny! You know Joe always finds the best in everything and he's bound to be a bit excited, his first day in a new job."

"You're probably right Luce, but I know I wouldn't like to be buried alive down there in the blackness."

"Stop being so melodramatic, Eva, and make me a cup of tea, will you, it's like the Sahara Desert in here."

At a quarter to nine, Eva made her way back into the playground. She watched as the children enjoyed their last moments of freedom before the bell summoned them into straight lines ready to file into the hall for assembly.

Over at the far end of the yard, a group of boys ranging in age from seven to eleven, had improvised goal posts from jumpers, and were fiercely engaged in a game of football, although each side seemed to be comprised of at least fifteen players. Some of the girls were skipping, chanting the same songs their mothers would have sung as children, dashing in and out of the turning ropes. Here and there, older girls, too 'grown-up' for such childish games, gathered in groups, chatting away nineteen to the dozen, as if they hadn't just seen each other yesterday.

Mavis Riley, Head Girl, walked purposefully to the middle of the yard and began to ring the brass bell vigorously. Order was restored out of chaos, as the children mustered in front of their respective class teachers. Eva surveyed the line of children in front of her. The youngest in the school, many hardly seemed big enough to be out on their own. Most of the girls had their long hair plaited, whereas the boys mimicked their fathers with short back and sides haircuts. Both were an effort to keep the dreaded nits at bay. Thank goodness for her new short hairstyle: it saved her at least five minutes in front of the mirror every morning.

Some, however, displayed signs of their impoverished backgrounds: unwashed and unkempt, dressed in ragged clothes, one or two didn't even have a pair of shoes to their name. At first, Eva had felt so sorry for these children that she had procured warm clothes and sound shoes for them to wear. Miss Alsopp, one of the older lady teachers, had informed her, not unkindly, that this was a waste, not only of her time but also of her meagre wages. "Their parents, by and large, are drunkards and wastrels. They will simply sell the things you give the children for a bottle of beer or an afternoon of 'pitch and toss'." Eva sought other ways to help these poorest of children, usually managing to slip them some nourishing food when most of the others went home for their midday meal.

Eva particularly liked morning assembly: to listen to the children's sweet voices raised in song; to watch their heads bowed, hands together, in prayer, filled her heart. Unfortunately, today's chosen hymn was 'All Things Bright and Beautiful' bringing tears to her eyes as she thought of Joe hard at work down the deep, dark mine. 'Yay though I walk through the valley of death...' the sombre tones of The Lord's Prayer, always the last prayer of the morning, brought her back to reality and she prepared to lead her class out of the hall to their classroom.

Still unable to keep her mind from straying, Eva decided something simple should be the order of the day. Settling the children quickly behind their desks, Eva instructed her monitors to give out the slates, pencils and rags. Carefully, she began writing the letters of the alphabet on the blackboard: Aa, Bb, Cc. "Tommy Naisbett! Don't forget I have eyes in the back of my head!" Tommy stopped trying to pull the plait of the girl in front of him, picked up his slate pencil and, with his tongue sticking out of the side of his mouth in concentration, began to copy his letters.

Eva was glad when the bell signalled the break for lunch; at last she could escape the classroom. Swiftly bypassing the staffroom, she left the school by the side entrance; she was in no mood for company. Once out of the playground, she slowed her step, making her way home along Church Street. The pavements gently steamed as the sun broke through the clouds.

Bella was waiting for her in the kitchen. She had

prepared cottage pie, her favourite. "Your father isn't in for lunch today so I thought we could eat in here for a change."

Eva hung her coat and hat up in the hall, then went through to her mother. She felt like a small child again, lost and alone, and was quite ready to welcome a little motherly cossetting. She took her place at the table as Bella dished out the pie and poured tea into her cup. Never one for beating about the bush, Bella dispensed with the niceties and got straight to the point. "I hope you haven't been moping about all morning Eva. I know you're thinking of Joe but worrying isn't going to help anyone."

"I can't help it, Mam. I hate to think of him down there in the cold and the dark. What makes it worse is, I know he's only doing it for me."

"Oh, is that a fact, young lady? I think you'll find Joe is doing it just as much for himself so that you can both be together. Is that not so?"

"Well, if you put it like that…" began Eva.

"The way you can help him most is by being grateful and proud of him instead of walking around with a face as long as a fiddle, glowering at everyone." Eva was about to interrupt but Bella went on. "Why don't you get ready after dinner tonight and we'll take a walk over to Ginny's. I'm sure I promised to take her some of my Damson jam. Now let's see you eat some of that pie before it goes cold."

Although Eva knew she would probably continue to think about Joe for the rest of the day, at least now she had something to look forward to and this brightened her mood considerably. Bella was relieved to see her daughter eating again and laughed with her as she chatted about what the children had got up to that morning.

"I'd better be getting back. The children have been so good this morning, I think we'll get the paints out this afternoon, although some of them will end up with more on their clothes than on the paper. I may be a little late, Mam, but with any luck Lucy will help me to clear away."

And then she was gone, with a smile on her face and a spring in her step.

CHAPTER EIGHT

Joe didn't have a watch. It had never mattered to
him before; he had always been able to tell the time
by the sun in the sky or the rising of the moon.
Down the pit, however, there was no way of
knowing how quickly or slowly time passed so it
was a relief when Eddy Dowling appeared and told
him it was time to knock off.

Bone weary, he led Benji back to his stall in the
underground stable. Joe stripped him of his limbers
and bridle, running his hands over the pony's sides
and legs, checking for any injuries or sore spots.
The young lad he'd seen earlier fetched him some
water to wash the pony down and then he dried him
off with straw. Putting his hand deep into his
pocket, he retrieved the apple Ginny had given him
for his bait. "There you go lad, I reckon you deserve
this more than I do." As the pony crunched the
apple, Joe rubbed behind his ears fondly. "I reckon
we're gonna make a good team, you and me." He
left Benji feeding contentedly and made his way
back down the tunnels to the shaft bottom.

By the time Joe reached the shaft, many of the other
miners were already assembled, keen to be in the
first cage up to bank. The onsetter rapped them
away and they rose swiftly, the force of the

acceleration bending their legs until they neared the braking zone then it felt almost as if they were floating. Blackened and grimed by the coal face, they emerged like moles squinting into the sunlight, laughing and joking, relieved to have survived another day.

Joe followed their lead, giving the banksman his other token, which would be paired with his first to mark his safe return to the surface. Then he handed his lamp in at the lamp cabin. The fresh air had never tasted sweeter. High above the fields beyond the pit yard a skylark sang a hymn more glorious than any sung in church.

He was hardly surprised to find Bob Stirling waiting by the gates.

"Well then Joe, what's tha make of that? Will ye be comin' back the morn?"

Joe grinned, his teeth and eyes shining brightly against the coaldust on his face. "Aye, I reckon there's worse places, Bob, but I don't think I'm ever gonna love the place. See you tomorrow." He was one of them now and surprisingly proud to be so. He joined the rest of the miners as they made their way wearily home through the streets of colliery houses, some to wives, some straight into the nearest public house where half-filled pints of beer would be standing waiting to be topped off.

All Joe wanted to do was to get home to his dinner: he could never remember being so hungry in his life. Tomorrow he'd have to see if Ginny had a metal tin to put his bait in; he wasn't letting the mice have it again. And he'd have to make sure he took two apples, one for him and one for Benji. Despite his fatigue, the thought of his new friend brought a smile to his face. The brave little pony had worked so hard and so willingly all shift, hauling tubs full of gear and props in bye to the faces and hauling full tubs of coal out again; never once refusing to do his bidding. He could see why Eddy Dowling held them in such high esteem.

His back ached as some of the tunnels were just high enough to let the ponies through and Joe, being six feet tall, had to bend almost double to navigate them. The heavy leather boots would serve him well, he could see that, but until they were 'worked in' he might have to put up with a few blisters. Still, all in all, it had been a good day, full of interesting new experiences, and the camaraderie of the miners was a feeling to be prized.

Stopping halfway up the hill, he could see their cottage. Smoke curled lazily out of the chimney. Below it, Joe knew, Ginny's pans would be bubbling away merrily full of … taties or puddings or broth? Whatever awaited him, Joe thought it just might be the most delicious meal he had ever tasted or would taste again. So long as there was lashings of gravy and loaves of Ginny's fine fresh bread.

Ginny heard him whistling long before she could see him coming up the lane. The tin bath was standing in front of the fire, ready to have the final kettle of scalding water added to it. She heard him stop to take off his boots before coming through the back door. She was relieved to see the smile on his face but she couldn't help but laugh at the state of him. "Mebbe I'd better get the scrubbing brush, our Joe, else you'll never get clean with plain old soap and water."

Joe chuckled, making a dive towards his sister. "Haven't you got a cuddle for your little brother, then, back from the dangers of the darkest Hell known to man?"

"You keep your distance or I'll give you hell, Joseph Fishburn. Now, get those clothes off so I can dad them outside while you have your bath. Are you hungry?"

Joe continued stripping off his shirt and trousers as he turned to look for the pan on the range. "Aye, I could eat a hoss, but better not let Benji hear me say that or he'll be going on strike."

"I take it Benji's the name of your pony. Well you can tell me all about it after you get that muck off you and you'd best make sharp 'cos there's a pie crust in the oven, taties and veg in the pan and it tastes better if it's not burnt." With that Ginny gathered up the dirty clothes, holding them at arm's length and made her way out into the yard where she would hang them over the line and hit them with a stick to knock as much coal dust and sweat out of them as she could manage, ready for the next day.

Meanwhile, Joe lowered himself into the steaming water, generously soaped the flannel and began to scour his body clean. Ginny had left a loofah ready so he could reach to scrub his back without the indignity of having to depend on his big sister. Some of the older miners refused to wash their backs during the week, saying it weakened them, but he would do his best to make sure he didn't carry the stink of the pit with him when he hopefully went to meet Eva later that night. He had so much to tell her. The smell of the rabbit pie in the oven spurred him on and he was soon out of the bath, towelled down and into his clean clothes left handy on the pulley maid. By the time Ginny came back in, even she could hear his stomach rumbling.

"Sit yourself down, Joe, and I'll get you a mug of tea. You must be famished."

Joe sat down by the fire and stretched his legs out on the hearth while Ginny busied herself putting out the dinner. The table was already set and she cut him a huge slice of golden pie crust, followed by steaming chunks of tender rabbit and slices of black pudding. Potatoes, carrots and cabbage followed in quick succession, the whole lot smothered with rich brown gravy. "I dare say you'd like some bread to go with that," but when Ginny turned around, she found Joe sound asleep in his chair. "Eee lad, it's a hard lesson you've learned today and that's no mistake. I reckon your dinner'll keep for a minute or two."

She covered his plate with another and set it by the fire to keep warm then she sat herself down in her chair on the opposite side of the range to watch over him while he slept.

CHAPTER NINE

A bedraggled Sunday morning crept quietly in. Joe, exhausted at the end of his first week down the mine, slept on oblivious to the time. Ginny, up at five as usual, had already fed and watered the animals and was busy milking Jenny, the goat, when Joe finally rose from his bed at seven. Making his way out to the stable, he watched on smiling as his sister, her head pressed against Jenny's side, expertly pulled on the teats to let down the milk; the swish of the liquid into the metal pail providing the rhythm as she softly crooned a soothing song.

"You should have given me a shout," Joe protested.

"You deserved a lie-in this once. I'm almost done, then you can turn these two out into the field while I get you some breakfast." Ginny lifted the pail of milk easily, placing a lid on top and leaving it by the door. "I'll make some cheese with that later. Jimmy Bell is partial to a bit of goat's cheese and he'll swap it for some butter from one of his cows."

Joe led Samson and Jenny out of the stable, across the lane and through the gate to the meadow. He took a moment to stretch his back and to drink in the sweet smell of the grass as the sun warmed the land.

Back in the kitchen, meanwhile, Ginny had scalded a fresh pot of tea and was cutting thick rashers from a flitch of bacon. She placed them into a frying pan heating on the fire. The sizzle immediately sent up an enticing aroma. The table was already laid with plates, cutlery and fresh bread and Joe sat down and began slicing himself a couple of doorstops from the loaf as Ginny poured their tea.

"I'll get a couple of hours in on the vegetable patch before church, Ginny. I should get the beans planted and mebbe put in another couple of rows of late taties."

"Well just make sure you leave enough time to get ready for church. Don't go showing up with soil under your fingernails. And remember, we've been invited up to the Greenall's for tea."

"As if I could forget! I hope Eva's dad doesn't give us too hard a time. You know how easy he can get Eva's temper up."

"Don't worry, I'm sure Bella will have everything under control. Now if you're finished get out from under my feet and let me get on."

Joe left the cottage whistling. Today was going to be a good day.

Reverend Shepherd had been preaching at Saint Mary's Church for longer than some of his parishioners could remember. Almost eighty, his face, etched with lines of experience, rarely showed the tiredness and frustration he sometimes felt as he approached the end of his ministry. Casting a benevolent eye over the congregation seated before him, he thought back to how many of them he had baptised, confirmed or married over the years. Seated to his right was Ben Fairbrother, his curate, who would take over his role when he completed his training later that year.

As people began to suffer under the stress of worsening economic conditions, many were becoming harsh in their treatment of their fellow man. He had decided to base his sermon on Matthew 7:1 'Judge not, that ye be not judged' although as numbers attending church were falling, he doubted he would reach the worst offenders in the community.

As his sermon ended, he noticed his Church Warden, Thomas Greenall, looking rather sheepish. Maybe Tom had been forced to examine his own attitude towards young Joseph Fishburn, who had, it was rumoured, set his sights on Eva, his daughter. Certainly, the pair seemed unable to take their eyes off each other, even when their heads were supposed to be bowed in prayer. Maybe he could manage one more marriage before he hung up his surplus.

As the first hymn: 'Morning has broken', ended, Eva shepherded the Sunday School children down the aisle and across into the Church Hall. Most of them she knew from school but one or two of the older children were unfamiliar to her. Freed from the confines of the church, the children at once began to chatter and laugh amongst themselves. The tables in the hall were set out with paper and colouring crayons. Eva told them the story of 'The Good Samaritan' and then they drew a picture in response to it.

After church, Eva and Joe wandered aimlessly around the churchyard, while Bella and Ginny sorted out the afternoon's arrangements.

"Do you think your Dad knows why we are coming to tea, Eva?"

"Of course, he does, silly, although he hasn't said a word about it to me."

"Well just let me handle it. You know how easy you lose your temper sometimes."

"I do not!" Eva retorted heatedly, immediately looking shamefaced.

"That's exactly what I mean, Eva. If you get his back up, he'll never agree to us courting, will he? So, for once bite your tongue," Joe grinned, "then I can kiss it better for you later."

Eva laughed, then turned as her mother called to her. "I will be the epitome of a dutiful daughter."

Joe wasn't entirely sure he knew what she was talking about but he got the gist anyway. "See you this afternoon at four, and don't be late! Coming Mam!" One thing Joe was certain of: life would never be dull with Eva around.

Later, in the Greenall's dining room, Joe squirmed in his seat. His shirt collar chafed his neck, his jacket felt too tight and his tongue was sticking to the roof of his mouth. At the head of the table, Tom was also feeling uncomfortable. He knew why they were gathered around his dining table and despite Bella's reassurances, he still found it difficult to reconcile his feelings about the young man before him. How could he entrust his little girl to this hawker?

Bella broke into his thoughts. "Tell me, Joe, how did you find your first week down the mine? Is it as bad as they say?"

"It will take some getting used to: it's cold and dark and dirty but the men have welcomed me and watch out for me where they're able. They're a fine crowd and I'm proud to be one of them." Steadfastly he held Tom's gaze. "I understand you come from mining stock yourself, Mr. Greenall."

Tom cleared his throat noisily before replying, "That's right Joseph, but I can't say my father ever gave me cause to be proud of him."

"I suppose you know that my dad was killed in an explosion down the pit when I was nowt but a bairn," Joe continued, "and my sister, Ginny, has made a marvellous job of bringing us all up. There's no finer lady in Wain Hill and no harder worker." Ginny, embarrassed by her brother's outburst, blushed crimson.

"We all have the greatest regard for your sister, Joe, she is a woman of the finest integrity and I can only hope you will prove yourself her match."

"I will do my level best to make everyone proud of me, Mr. Greenall, and that is why I have come here today to formally ask you if me and Eva can step out together."

"I can't say I am entirely happy about the situation, Joe, but never let it be said that I won't give any man the chance to prove himself. So long as my wife and your sister are agreeable, as I am sure they are, then you have my consent. But be warned, if you hurt Eva in any way you will regret the day you were born."

"Now Tom stop, before you frighten the poor lad to death. I am sure they both realise how serious you take your fatherly duties. Right, now that's over, perhaps we can enjoy our tea. Sponge cake, anyone? Although you will find it a poor imitation of yours Ginny, it was fresh from the bakery yesterday."

A relieved ripple of laughter ran around the table, as everyone tucked into the sandwiches and cakes that had lain neglected. Under the table Joe felt the comforting touch of Eva's toe on his foot.

CHAPTER TEN

Sundays were spent in long walks and visits to nearby landmarks. The young couple became especially fond of Durham with its gentle meandering river and narrow cobbled streets leading up to the sanctuary of the cathedral. Within the shelter of its cloisters they strolled arm in arm, each discovering the other; exploring likes and dislikes: what they had in common and what made them different. In secluded places, they lay on the river banks disturbed only by rowers sculling skilfully over the water.

All too soon Summer faded, evenings drew in, wrapping chilly fingers around them. As September melted into October, rains dampened spirits, chasing them indoors. Winds tugged at their clothes so that they hugged their coats closer and held onto their hats.

November was an easier time on the small holding. Cleared vegetable pots were dug over and left to the frosts to do their work. The animals sheltered in the warmth of their stable and sties, safe from snow and frost. Hens and ducks laid less often. Everyone, it seemed, was settling down to endure the Winter; the world held its breath, waiting for the return of Spring.

When the weather became too fierce, Joe and Eva took refuge in Ginny's front room, the door left discreetly open, while Bella and Ginny drank tea by the fire. Joe continued to work at the pit and Eva taught her classes. Life went on.

At the mine, however, all was not well. There was talk amongst the men that Number 2 District would soon be closed down. Production had been falling steadily until it was no longer viable. Everyone knew that it would mean layoffs. It looked like being a poor Christmas for some. Worried, Joe sought out his mentor, Bob Stirling.

"Have you heard who's to be let go, Bob?"

"Not yet, lad, but I'll not kid ya, it's generally last in, first out," the little man pulled a wry face. "Mebbe the best thing you can do is transfer to another pit afore there's others looking for work."

"But everywhere round here is in the same boat, Bob. Just the other day in The Wheatsheaf, word was that Wain Hill will be closed entirely before the end of the decade and Brampton might follow.

"Aye it's sad times round here, that's for sure but nothing lasts forever. They reckon the big pits ower on the coast is the future now. Leave it with me and I'll ask about and see what I can find out."

"Thanks Bob, yer a good marra. I'd best get away or I'll miss the cage but I'll come and see ye tomorrow."

Bob watched Joe's retreating back as he crossed the yard to the lamp cabin, his shoulders hunched, head down. It pained him to see the young lad so down. Meanwhile, Joe was deep in thought. His sister Ellen's husband, Jack, worked over at Essingham; he'd see if he'd heard if there were any jobs going there. Maybe he could get set on, on the faces; facework paid much better and he would save as much as he could so that he and Eva could marry.

Eva was not quite so keen. Joe's moving away was fraught with danger. They would hardly see each other and the old adage 'out of sight, out of mind,' haunted her.

"What if he meets someone else, Mam? Someone more attractive than me?"

Bella resisted the urge to smile; this was no laughing matter to her daughter, although she thought she was overreacting to the situation. "Calm down, Eva, he hasn't even gone anywhere yet. And if finding work elsewhere is Joe's only option then so be it."

"But …"

"No ifs or buts about it my girl. I'm sure Joe loves you and if you love him then you will have to trust him. Or do you think he's some fly- by- night who is simply out to take advantage of a silly young girl?"

Eva was stunned: suddenly she was the one in the wrong and certainly not the recipient of sympathy as she expected. She couldn't help but break out into a laugh; her mother had certainly turned the tables on her. "Well I guess that puts me in my place, Mam. Of course, I trust Joe, but I will miss him dreadfully."

"No more than he will miss you, I'm sure, but if you do love each other then you will both have to make sacrifices, won't you? So, let's have no more feeling sorry for yourself, Joe needs you to be strong."

By the end of November, Joe's future had been settled. With the help of Bob Stirling and his brother-in-law, Jack, he had secured a job as canchman at Essingham Colliery. The work was hard and dangerous, developing and making safe the roadways servicing the faces, but Joe was delighted with the subsequent increase in his possible earnings.

His sister, Ellen, had arranged for him to board with the Widow Evans, who lived next door. She had lost her husband in a bad accident down the pit two years ago and would be glad of the company as well as the extra income.

The final few days before he was due to leave were tense as the young couple fought to come to terms with their separation. They had become used to seeing each other almost every day and Eva could hardly bear to think of the long days without him.

Sitting in Ginny's front room that night, Eva clung desperately to him, their kisses more fervent and passionate than ever.

"It won't be so bad, Eva, not now I've got a bike. I'll be able to get back most weekends and you'll have your teaching to keep you occupied while I'm gone."

"I know I'm being selfish, Joe, but I really wish you didn't have to go. I'm going to miss you so much."

"It won't be for too long; I'll save every penny I can. One day we'll be together, I promise."

If Ginny and Bella noticed anything strange later about the happy demeanour of the pair as they emerged from the parlour, they refrained from remarking upon it, only allowing a knowing look to pass between them.

Later, as Ginny and Joe sat companionably by the

fire, she retrieved a small box from her pocket and held it out to her brother. Gently opening it, he was amazed to find a solitaire diamond ring within.

"I don't understand; where did this come from? It's beautiful and must have cost a small fortune."

"It was mine," Ginny answered gazing wistfully into the glowing coals. "Edwin gave me it just before he went to the front for the last time." A tear rolled slowly down her cheek.

Joe could just remember Ginny's young man who had been killed in the Great War but he had never realised they had become engaged to be married.

"We never got the chance of happiness, Joe, and I don't want you and Eva to wait a moment longer than necessary to be together. I know it can be a dangerous business working down the pits and God forbid anything should happen but if it did at least you would know true happiness if you were married first."

"But I can't take this, Gin, it must be all you have left of Edwin."

"I've got my memories. No-one can take those away, and if this can help you and Eva make memories of your own then it'll serve a much better purpose than stuck away in my dressing table drawer. Give it to Eva when you're ready or, if you think she might be offended by it, sell it and use the money to buy her a new one."

Speechless, Joe rose and wrapped his arms around his sister, hugging her tightly. Once again, she was putting herself last as she had done since their parents had died.

"I'll never be able to repay you for all you've done, Ginny. I won't ask Eva to marry me until I know that I can provide for her but hopefully this new job will be the answer to my prayers."

Standing in the firelight, Ginny thought of the handsome young man who had given his life for his country. Edwin, she knew, would have supported her actions and bestowed his blessing on the couple.

CHAPTER ELEVEN

Joe halted his bike at the top of the hill. It was still early and his breath steamed in the crisp morning air. He had left the cottage at seven, just as the first streaks of dawn appeared in the east, avoiding another farewell scene with Eva. Taking his father's old pit watch from his vest pocket, he checked it. Almost nine, he had made good time despite the ramshackle nature of the old delivery bike he rode. It had been a welcome gift from Eva's dad not just because it would save him many hours of walking, but also because it meant that Thomas seemed to be coming around to accepting him and Eva as a couple. St Mary's church bells startled him from his reverie. Mounting his bike, he set off down the hill towards Essingham Colliery; it would be a much easier ride from here on.

From the top of Seaside Lane, the colliery village was spreading out like an inkblot on the landscape. Behind the main parade of shops, terraced colliery houses were laid out in identical rows to the North, South and East, and this is how the areas came to be known. Unlike the neighbouring villages of Hawdene and Blackwell whose streets were known simply by numbers, 1st, 2nd, 3rd and so on, each street in Essingham had been named. The streets in the North area all began with A, those in South with

B and those in East with C. Where the road made a
sharp right at the bottom of the main street, Seaside
Lane, it became Station Road, quite simply because
it lead to the railway station located on the other
side of the railway track.

On the outskirts of each of these areas were the
miner's allotments whose possession was prized
greatly by families because they not only provided a
wealth of fresh produce to feed growing families
but also a welcome respite for men who spent much
of their lives underground. Out in the fresh air men
planted their crops of potatoes, onions and
cabbages, taking pleasure in watching them grow.
Many also kept chickens mainly for their eggs and
some had built pigeon lofts from which they flew
their birds in races all over the country, even as far
away as France. In the annual Leek Show,
competition was fierce as men vied for the coveted
Best in Show title.

Jack and Ellen had set up home in Bourne Street,
South. The house was small consisting of a living
room/kitchen and scullery downstairs, two
bedrooms upstairs and a coalhouse and toilet at the
bottom of the back yard. Although they had only
been married for two years they already had one
baby, Alice, and another on the way hence there
was no room for Joe to stay with them. But the
Widow Evans, who lived next door, had been a

good friend to Ellen when they had moved into the street and she had been only too willing to take Joe in.

Jean Evans thought it would be nice to have a man about the house again: someone to cook and clean for, leaving his boots in the way and generally filling the place with nuisance. At fifty-two, Jean Evans was considered too old for most paid employment. True, as a widow, she was allowed to remain in her house rent free and continued to receive a reduced coal allowance, but it was still hard to manage on nothing but a widow's pension. The extra income from a paying lodger would be most welcome.

As Joe turned into the street he could see his sister's face at the window of Number 23. Before he had time to dismount, the door burst open and she was dashing across the grass verge to greet him. Flinging her arms about his neck, she kissed him soundly on the cheek, then hugged him close. "Hello Baby Brother, it's so good to see you. I was beginning to think you had forgotten us!"

Struggling to free himself from her vice like arms, Joe planted a kiss on top of his sister's head, for she was at least six inches shorter than him. At twenty-six, Ellen retained her youthful looks: her cheeks flushed with pleasure, eyes, brown like Joe's, danced with merriment. Slender, despite her pregnancy. "Will you put me down, woman? You'll have the street out gawking at your new fancy man."

"I might have a word or two to say about that!" Jack emerged with Alice in his arms. "She's been like a cat on hot bricks since afore seven. Anyone would think the King himself was paying us a visit."

Joe shook Jack's hand warmly. "Good to see you, Jack. I'll never be able to thank you enough for getting me fixed up at the pit. I reckon it won't be long before most of the mines over by Durham will be worked out, so there will be more and more men looking to move their families over here to the coast."

"There's no need to thank me, Joe, it would be a poor brother-in-law who'd see his wife's brother out of work when they're crying out for good men here to develop new districts out under the sea. You must be parched after cycling all that way. I suppose it's a bit early for the pub, so let's away in and have a cup of tea."

Just then the door to number twenty-two opened and out hopped Jean Evans. Neat as a new pin, everything about Jean appeared half-size. Her short mousy hair was permed into tight curls and she was dressed in a smart brown coat over a red blouse, obviously ready to attend Morning Service. In her forthright way, she approached Joe holding out her hand in greeting. "I'm very pleased to meet you, Joe."

As he shook Jean's tiny hand, his own felt huge and clumsy in contrast; he could feel how delicate were her bones. She reminded him of a bird, her head nodding constantly as she regarded him with interest. "Ellen's told me all about you," she chattered, "and all about your young lady too. You must bring her to meet me first chance you get." As she talked, she continuously hopped from one leg to the other.

Joe smiled, "I certainly will, Mrs. Evans, I'm sure you two will get along famously. We can't thank you enough for your kindness."

"Shush now, it's you who are doing me the favour, Joe. It will be nice to have some company around the house. There was only me and Bob, you see; we had no children and all our relations are long dead. But it hasn't been so lonely since these two moved in next door," she beamed at Ellen and Jack, "especially since little Alice was born, and now there's another one on the way; it just keeps on getting better. I'm off to church now but here's a key so you can let yourself in when you're ready. See you later." And then she was gone, bobbing up the street like a brave little robin.

"Well, Joe, what do you make of our neighbour; she's quite a character, isn't she?" Jack laughed as Joe stood mouth open, dumbfounded.

"I think we'll get along fine, Jack. She's certainly not shy of coming forward, is she?"

Ellen took Joe's arm. "Come along in, the tea's mashed and will be getting cold. I bet you wouldn't say no to a bacon sarnie, either."

"Thought you'd never ask," Joe quipped as he followed his sister into the house.

CHAPTER TWELVE

The South-East Durham coastline is notable for its series of deep ravines or denes that run inland from the coast. These denes separate the colliery villages of Essingham, Hawdene and Blackwell and their respective mines. At the top end of South, where Ellen and Jack lived, there was a sheer limestone cliff remaining from earlier quarrying, which marked the boundary of this area and above this lay Paradise Gardens, divided into allotments. Jack was keen to show Joe what he had achieved in the last year since he had acquired his own allotment and suggested he accompany him when he went to feed his hens.

Although he was feeling content after his satisfying breakfast of bacon, eggs, sausage and black pudding, Joe was keen to see what the land had to offer in so industrial a landscape. They walked in silence, preferring to save their breath for the steady climb up the steep path that lead to the gardens.

Paradise was well named, thought Joe, as they emerged into a land still green despite the harsh cold. Each allotment, neatly fenced from its neighbours, revealed a wealth of crops ready to sustain the miners through the long Winter. Leeks, parsnips, Brussel sprouts and kale waited to be harvested; where the earth lay bare, the soil had been roughly dug over; the Winter frosts would break it down further. Almost every allotment had some sort of shed built from whatever had come to hand; some sported handsome pigeon lofts, liveried in a variety of colours striped with white; several boasted home-made greenhouses, some with heaters fuelled by coal, so even here there was the tang of smoke in the air.

Standing on the edge of the quarry Joe could see for miles; the wind, straight off the sea, whipping his face with icy fingers. Out on the water, a coaster battled through white horses, making its way determinedly North to the Wear or the Tyne. Inshore a tiny cobble was being tossed about like flotsam, its occupant gallantly pulling up crab pots.

 Joe nodded towards it, "Rather him than me."

"There's a few huts down in Boatman's Bay," Jack informed him. "A few of the lads set pots and they have to be tended everyday whatever the weather. Not my idea of fun either, although I did go out with one of them in the Summer."

"Well, I'll be keeping my feet firmly on the ground. But I might be interested in getting one of these allotments, Jack. How do I go about it?"

"You have to put your name down; there's quite a

long waiting list I'm afraid. But you can always share mine; there's plenty of work for two."

They had turned along a narrow pathway and came to a wooden gate. Jack removed the padlock and pushed it back so Joe could enter. Joe was impressed with the orderliness: the garden had been divided into distinct sections, each edged with large stones, separated by trodden paths.

At the far end of the plot, there stood a long wooden shed from which emanated a throaty clucking. The last quarter of the structure housed a store for tools and feed. Jack retrieved a hessian sack and entered the hen house. At once the birds flocked to him as he filled a trough with meal. "Can you fill us a can of water from the butt, please, Joe?"

Joe did as he was bid, then entered the shed behind Jack. "I've never seen hens as small as these; what are they?"

"They're bantams, good layers even at this time of year." Jack was checking the nesting boxes for eggs as he talked. "Here put a couple of these in your pocket and Jean'll likely boil them for your breakfast tomorrow."

"Things are looking up," Joe thought, as he carefully wrapped the warm brown eggs in his handkerchief. He might be missing Eva but there was plenty going on to fill the empty hours between shifts. He retrieved a fork from the shed and began to turn over the clods of earth in one of the plots, smashing the lumps until they were reduced to a fine tilth. There was nothing like hard graft for getting your mind sorted.

Jack watched bemused as Joe put his back into it, accompanying his efforts by whistling 'Cheek to Cheek.'

By the time the men got home, Ellen was ready to dish up Sunday dinner. The aroma of roast beef greeted them as they kicked their boots off at the back door.

"I thought hunger would bring you both home on time," Ellen grinned. "Do you want your puddings with your veg, Joe, or would you prefer them before with gravy from the meat?"

"Just put everything on the plate together, please. I don't want too much after that big breakfast."

While the men washed at the sink, Ellen finished laying the cutlery and cruet on the crisp white tablecloth that now protected the green chenille cloth covering the table. She piled roast beef and Yorkshire puddings onto plates, accompanied by roast and mashed potatoes, carrots, swede, cabbage and steeped peas, all slathered with delicious onion gravy. Just the job to chase out the cold. They ate in silence until every plate was clean, not a morsel remained.

Ellen rose to clear the dishes as the men took seats beside the fire. Jack took a pipe from the mantel, carefully clearing it before tamping down a new charge of tobacco which he lit from the fire with a spill. Settling back in his chair, he loosened his belt a notch and let out a deep sigh of contentment. "Thank God for Sundays, a day of rest."

Perfectly relaxed, Joe could feel the early morning start threatening to overtake him. With a full belly, the pungent smell from Jack's pipe and the warmth of the coal fire, he was minutes from drifting into a deep sleep.

"You'd better get yourself into next door, before you nod off." His sister's voice brought him back sharply to the present. "Jean likes a lie down of a Sunday afternoon and will be waiting on you." Dragging himself from his chair, Joe collected his bag and made for the back door, giving Ellen his thanks and a kiss on the cheek on the way.

CHAPTER THIRTEEN

Through the kitchen window Eva contemplated the garden. The shrubs and lawn were bathed in weak wintry sunshine but they did little to lift her spirits. Joe was gone, just like the flowers of summer, all the colour seemed to have faded away. Church too had been grey and forbidding, empty without him. She knew that she was being melodramatic but she could not ignore the ache in her heart.

"You'll wear the pattern off that plate if you wash it many more times," Bella had crept up unnoticed behind her. "Joe hasn't been gone above a few hours and you're mooning about like a lovesick calf." She was worried about her daughter; she was too quiet. "C'mon love, you will get used to his being away, you know. The best thing you can do is keep busy so the days pass more quickly. Why don't you take a walk over to see Ginny, I'm sure she's missing him too."

Eva didn't make it to the cottage that night. By the time she had finished the washing up and put all the Sunday dishes away it was already dusk. Instead she took herself up to her room; she wasn't in the mood for small talk or her father's somewhat tactless comments. If she couldn't talk to Joe, then she would write to him; not sad dreary letters but ones filled with funny anecdotes and as much love as she could convey. She knew it unlikely that she would receive a missive back, Joe was not given to putting pen to paper, but that didn't matter. Writing might help ease the loneliness.

Dear Joe,

I know it is only a few short hours since we parted but already it seems like a lifetime. I hope you did not find the journey to Essingham too arduous and that Ellen, Jack and little Alice are all well.

By the time you read this you will have begun work down the pit. When you come home you can tell me all about it and about your new landlady. Is she a dragon? Can she cook as well as Ginny? I doubt it!

Although everyone complains that I have been moping about the house like a lovesick calf, I have decided I must be brave and not snap at people so much, especially Father, who is totally baffled by my present behaviour. When you return, hopefully quite soon, you will find me a cheerful companion full of the latest news and gossip.

Sitting in our usual pew in church this morning, I was ignorant of Reverend Shepherd's sermon, preferring to sit thinking of you. Gazing forlornly across the aisle, I noticed that Mister Snow must also be finding the Reverend difficult to follow because he was starting to nod off. At the very moment the good vicar said, "Let us pray," the old man let out a tremendous snort and almost jumped over his pew in shock. Even some of the older members of the congregation found difficulty in smothering their laughter. The young Cassidy twins did not help the matter when they decided to extend the joke by grunting like pigs. Reverend Shepherd was almost apoplectic as he turned his fierce gaze upon them and harrumphed loudly to show his displeasure.

Later at lunch, Father remarked that it was unfortunate that this was the only time he had seen me smile all day. I wonder what he would say if he knew the reason I smiled was not so much the incident, although it was quite funny, but thinking of how you would have enjoyed it.

That's all for now Joe, I suppose I will have to join the others in the sitting room to listen to something dreadfully old-fashioned on the radio.

Sleep well my darling and know that I am thinking of you every minute of the day and night.

Your ever loving,

Eva x

As Eva made her way downstairs her tread was a little lighter. Writing the letter had almost been like talking to Joe as she tried to imagine him sitting alone in his tiny room, bored and lonely.

Of course, she couldn't have known that this was very far from the truth. After tea Joe and Jean Evans had been invited into Ellen's, together with a young married couple, Tom and Ada, who lived in the next street, for a game of cards and a little liquid refreshment procured from the carry-out at The Station Hotel, known locally as The Trust. Despite feeling somewhat guilty, Joe enjoyed himself immensely, even though he didn't even win one hand of Gin Rummy.

Lying on his bed that evening, he stared at the moon through his open curtains. Was Eva looking at the same moon? She would be teaching in her classroom the next day, while he would be underground in a strange pit, amongst strange workmates. And what of Ginny? Would she turn into an old maid with no-one to fuss over? Finally, he drifted into sleep.

Bella rolled over and rested her hand on Thomas's chest. "What's troubling you? You've been tossing and turning for the last half hour."

Thomas lay his hand gently on top of his wife's. "I'm worried about our Eva. She's been so quiet today. I know she's missing that lad but I guess I just didn't realise how much they love each other. Have I been an old fool, Bel?"

"No more than usual Tom," Bella replied. "Don't go worrying yourself into an early grave over those two. It won't do them any harm to cool off for a while."

"But what if I've driven them apart? What if he doesn't come back? She'll never forgive me."

Bella sat up and looked her husband full in the face. "If he doesn't come back, and I'd say there's little likelihood of that, then he can't really love her, can he? So she would be better off without him, wouldn't she?"

"I suppose you're right better a short sharp shock now than harsher heartache later."

Bella took Thomas's face in her hands and shook her head sadly. "Oh Tom you fond old fool, of course Joe will be back, first chance he gets if I know him. It might take them a while but I'm sure everything will work out for them in the long run. Meanwhile, can you try to cheer the lass up instead of wearing a face as long as hers?"

She kissed him deeply, pushing him gently back onto the pillows, his arms automatically enclosing her as he drew her to him; they were soon lost in their own passion.

CHAPTER FOURTEEN

Joe reported to the lamp cabin at eight the next morning. A poor night had left him feeling a bit groggy when he rose at six, but Jean Evans had done him proud with a hearty breakfast of bacon and eggs, washed down with a mug of strong tea. His bait lay ready in its tin on the sideboard next to his water bottle, so that all he had to do was don his old jacket over his pit clothes and set off for his first shift at Essingham, a mere five minutes' walk away. A pity Jack was not in the same shift, he thought.

"Joe, is it? Joe Fishburn?" A tall upright man, about forty, approached him hand outstretched in greeting.

"Aye that's me." At six feet, it was rare that Joe could look a fellow miner straight in the eye. He took the man's hand, surprised at the strength of the grip. "Pleased to meet you, err.."

"Stan Barlow. I'll be showing you around, you're to be on my team. I see you've got your lamp and tokens so let's get ower to the shaft. With a bit of luck we'll catch the first cage down."

Stan talked as they walked. He was still a handsome man, with deep blue eyes set above a straight nose and square, cleft chin, he must have had all the lasses after him in his younger days. Joe was finding it difficult to match him stride for stride.

Despite his previous experience, Joe felt out of place; after all he knew few people here and everything about Essingham pit was much more modern than Brampton. Sunk at the turn of the century, the first coal was drawn in 1910. Everything seemed bigger: the wheels and buildings towered over the open pit yard. When they reached the cage, Joe found there was not one but three decks stacked on top of each other. Handing his token to the banksman, he was frisked for contraband, then allowed to enter the bottom cage; the men were still packed in like sardines, however.

Within minutes the cage was full and they were dropping rapidly through the darkness. Joe felt the familiar lurch in his stomach and had to force himself to breathe as they plummeted down the shaft. Slowing down, light appeared as they approached the Low Main and the men were disgorged into the tunnels to begin their onward journey out under the sea.

As they marched along, Joe couldn't help but steal a glance or two up towards the roof; here they were thousands of feet below the surface; only their lamps keeping the total blackness at bay; the thud of their boots echoing around them. When you stopped for a moment, you could hear dripping as water forced its way out of the cracks in the rock. Joe shivered as he pictured the might of the North Sea rolling incessantly over them.

Soon they arrived at the deputy's kist where Joe was introduced to Bert Soulsby, the deputy who would be overseeing his shift. The rest of the team continued on to the coalface while Bert satisfied himself that Joe would cope with the duties of a canchman, one of the most dangerous jobs down the mine.

"Stan here will stay alongside you today. Just watch him and you'll soon pick up the ropes. Remember the men on the face rely on you to keep the gates up but safety comes first; their lives are in your hands."

For the first time Joe felt the weight of responsibility lying heavy on his shoulders. This was a far cry from his previous job as timber leader. If he had messed up there then it was only his own life and that of his pony at risk but now he had not only the lives of the face men but also the welfare of their wives and families depending on his every move; there could be no margin for error.

"Don't look so worried," Stan reassured him, "there's a tried and true way to tunnelling. Stick with me and you'll soon pick it up. If you're unsure about anything at all then ask. No second guessing down here."

"Right I'll leave you to it lads," said Bert as he collected his lamp hanging on the prop beside him. "I'll be back before you pull the props, Stan."

A cough came from somewhere behind Joe's shoulder. He turned and faced a short, rather stout man, fifty or thereabouts, with blue eyes so pale they were almost white. Stan introduced him as Fred, the third member of their team.

"This the new lad then, Stan?"

"Aye this is Joe. Joe meet Fred. Any questions, ask Fred. He's been on this job so long he's forgotten more than I'll ever know."

Fred gave Joe a quick nod as they briefly shook hands. "Right we need to get on up the maingate. Ten o'clock shift sorted the tailgate last night but the face advanced a fair way yesterday and it needs making safe before we can develop the roadway and lay the extra rails to get the coal out."

Reaching the entrance to the coal face, Fred was deployed to stop anyone coming off the face while the canch was dropped. The canch was the roof material which had to be brought down before the steel girders could be set in to support the raised roof more securely than the timber props already in place.

"Bert says you'll be ready to pull the props soon," a tousled haired lad appeared leading his pony. Stan showed Joe how to tie the ropes onto the props and the pony's limbers so the strength of the beast could pull the props out, keeping a relatively safe distance between themselves and the falling roof.

"You've got to keep your wits about you," Stan said seriously, "It's rare for all the stone to drop at once and the whole area can be treacherous until we get the supports back in." One look at the deadly earnestness on Stan's face brought home to Joe the danger of this operation. On Stan's signal Joe slapped the animal's rump smartly and the pony strained steadily against the ropes until the props gave way and were pulled free. An ominous cracking and crunching ensued as the roof gave way; several tons of grey slate stone thundered to the ground in front of them. Nervously he kept watch for any sign of danger as Stan moved in to dislodge any remaining broken stones with a long, metal crowbar.

At last Stan thought it safe enough to erect the three, steel arch girders to support the new roof. Wood was packed in to the gaps between the arching girder and the overhead stone. Joe already knew the value of using wood for this type of job: wood talked to you, giving you reassurance as the weight came on to squash it; you could see and hear it give as it took the strain.

Once all supports were safely in place, the boulders and debris were cleared away into the goaf, the area behind the advancing face, packed inside the butt wood supports. Many of the boulders and slabs of stone were so big they were impossible to move. Fred had rejoined them by then and their mel hammers rang out in unison as they reduced the stone to more manageable proportions. Stan informed Joe that it was normal for one canch drop per shift; this allowed the gates to keep up with the coal face. Coal would be transported down from the face via the main gate, while all materials for face development would come up through the tail gate.

At last Joe felt it was once again safe enough to breathe normally; without even realising it he had almost been holding his breath throughout the dangerous procedure. Sweat ran down his back; he was soaked through. Stan gave him a reassuring pat on the back. "Well done, marra. I guess you'll do." Stan had been impressed by the way Joe had maintained his vigilance, never once waivering in completing all tasks allotted to him.

"Here, you might like to keep this as a souvenir of your first shift as a canchman." Stan was holding out a piece of stone, "It's a fossil. That plant grew millions of years ago they reckon. Then over time it was turned to stone by the pressure."

Joe examined the fossil in the light from his lamp. There, embedded in the stone, he could clearly see a perfect impression of a fern. "I'll give it to Eva," he thought, "she'll likely want to show it to her class and give them a lesson on how the coal seams were formed all that time ago."

But he knew that there were many things to do with his job that he would never share with Eva: the true danger he would face every day; the way his nerves would pull tight each time they dropped the canch; the number of miners who had been badly lamed or killed under roof-falls.

Still, the money was good and he felt certain he would fit in well at Essingham. He might even get a few racing pigeons. He now felt certain that he and Eva would be married before another year was out. Life only got better!

CHAPTER FIFTEEN

Christmas was usually one of Eva's favourite times of year. The last week of school before the holiday was filled with seasonal activities. A tall tree graced the corner of the hall and every classroom was decorated from top to toe by the children. On Wednesday afternoon parents had been invited to watch the infants perform their Nativity Play and the Juniors sang carols in the evening.

The window of every shop on the High Street boasted a display overflowing with Christmas goods, none more so than Greenall's Grocers. Fancy tins of biscuits jostled for position amongst Christmas fruit cakes, jars of mincemeat and colourful boxes of chocolates. Inside, a vast range of cooked meats lay ready, together with round cheeses; some, like Stilton or Brie, adding a more exotic touch to everyday Cheddar and Cheshire.

The usual array of pills, potions and tonics had been cleared away from the window of the Chemist shop next door and had been replaced with gift sets of scented soaps, fine talcum powders and luxurious bath crystals. An empty bottle could be filled from a Sherry or Port cask for a shilling to grace the table with Christmas cheer.

Even the turkeys and gammons hanging in the butcher's window had been hung about with gaily coloured streamers to join the festive fun. Tray upon tray of meat from fine fillet steak to humble pork sausages promised feasting galore. It was hard to remember that for some Christmas would be a painful reminder of how little they had; how much they had to struggle to put the simplest meal on their table every day.

Eva, however, was not inclined to join in with the festivities. It was the Saturday before Christmas; school had broken up for the holidays the day before and it seemed there was little hope that she would get to see Joe soon. It had been three weeks since he had left and the weather had turned extremely cold; it seemed the snow and the wind conspired to keep them apart.

The bell gave out its familiar cheery ding as she opened the door to her father's shop but today it failed to raise a smile. Thomas was standing in his usual station behind the counter; a warm, brown overall his only concession to the cold. He smiled broadly at his daughter as she paused to wipe her feet on the mat.

"What brings you out on a day like today? Has your mother sent you on an errand?"

"Not really, although she did say to see if there's

some nice ham for tomorrow's tea. I thought I'd come down and give you a bit of a hand. It's bound to get busy the last Saturday before Christmas."

Thomas had to admit he would be grateful for some extra help but today there was another reason he was glad to see Eva. "It's a pity that lad of yours won't be coming home, lass."

Eva shrugged. "You know how he's fixed, Dad. Even if he could manage to bike over, he doesn't dare risk it in case we get more snow and he gets snowed up here and can't get back in time to start work again." Eva's face told Thomas how much she was missing Joe.

"Aye, I was talking to Ginny yesterday and she was saying how she's at a loose end since Joe's gone and how much she's missing him and the rest of the family. That cottage'll be a lonely place this Christmas I reckon."

"Do you think we could ask her over to spend Christmas Day with us, Dad?" Thomas smiled. His daughter might be suffering but she could still feel compassion for someone less fortunate.

"Oh, I think we can do one better than that, lass."

Eva had been absentmindedly rearranging the display of tinned fruit on the counter. She raised her head to study her father. "What do you mean, Dad?"

"I thought it might be nice to take the Morris out for a bit of a spin on Sunday and that I could drop Ginny over at their Ellen's."

Eva's face lit up. Racing around the end of the counter she hugged her father tightly. "There will be room for a little one in the back, won't there?" she beamed up at him.

"Oh, I can do one better than that young lady. Your Mam and Ginny have arranged it so Ginny can stay at Mrs Evans until Boxing Day. And, providing you don't mind sharing a bed, you can stay too."

Eva looked into her father's face. He surely wouldn't joke about something so important, would he? "But where will Joe stay? Mrs Evans only has two bedrooms."

"Joe will have to sleep on Ellen's settee for a couple of nights but I don't think you'll hear him complaining about that! The real stumbling block was getting Ginny to leave those blessed animals of hers. But Jimmy Bell says he will go round every day and feed them and milk the goat. If I didn't know better, I'd think Jimmy had his sights set on Ginny Fishburn.

"Well, what are you waiting for? I'm guessing you'll have a lot to do if you're to be ready first thing tomorrow."

Reaching up, Eva planted a resounding kiss on her father's cheek then was out of the door in a flash, her mind in a whirl. There was her suitcase to pack; was her blue dress clean? She would have a bath and wash her hair; after all there were no bathing facilities in the miners' houses. And she must find the time to buy presents for Ellen, Jack and little Alice; and Mrs. Evans of course. Oh dear, she had forgotten the ham! Never mind, her Dad might remember it. Now to pop into the toy shop. She was sure she had seen a delightful spinning top in their window last week; it would make a perfect present for Alice.

CHAPTER SIXTEEN

At ten o'clock exactly on Sunday morning, Thomas, Bella and Eva set off in the car to collect Ginny from her cottage. As they would only be staying until Boxing Day, Eva had managed to pack all she needed into a small leather suitcase. Her father had also loaded a wicker hamper, filled with Christmas goodies, which was destined for Mrs Evans as a thank you for allowing Eva and Ginny to stay.

Ginny must have been waiting with her hat and coat already on. Thomas hardly had time to sound his car horn when she was out of the door, laden with bags and boxes.

"What's all this then?" Thomas blustered. "I've got an automobile, you know, not an omnibus."

"It's just a few odds and ends I baked for our Ellen. Hardly anything at all. And if you must know that carpet bag has my bits and pieces in. We're not all rich enough to own posh luggage!"

"Now Ginny," Bella interjected, "you know Tom's only teasing. There's more than enough room for everything. Even the goat, if you'd a mind to bring her."

Once Ginny was settled on the back seat beside

Eva, they were off. Although there had been no snow overnight, it was bitterly cold and Thomas had to drive carefully to avoid the treacherous patches of ice on the roads. Thankfully the car had a heater but this meant Bella frequently had to clear the condensation from the windscreen with an old cloth so Thomas could see where he was going.

One hour later, they turned at last into Bourne Street, Thomas blaring his horn as he pulled up outside number twenty-three. The front door was flung open by Ellen and the women were ushered inside into the warm, Joe hugging Eva as if he might never let her go. Thomas and Jack retrieved all the luggage from the boot then hurriedly followed them.

The kettle sang quietly on the hob, the teapot ready to receive the boiling water. Eva noticed the improvements that had been made to the range in this relatively modern colliery house. Gone was the set pot, replaced by a back boiler behind the fire that heated the water and sent it directly to the hot water tap over the sink in the back kitchen.

Soon everyone had been divested of their outdoor clothes and settled down with a steaming cup of tea. Alice was quite happily sitting on Ginny's lap cuddling into her Aunt's ample bosom, sucking on her thumb. Ellen was obviously delighted to have her sister and Eva there for the holiday. "We can't thank you enough for bringing Ginny over Mr. Greenall. And I'm sure Joe is just as grateful to see Eva at last."

"Always glad to be of service. Anyway, I don't think we could have put up with Eva's miserable face all over Christmas, something had to be done."

Bella smiled her agreement. "You certainly look as if an extra pair of hands wouldn't come amiss, Ellen. When is the baby due?"

"Not 'til February, Mrs. Greenall, although Jack is worried I might not last 'til then," Ellen laughed squeezing her husband's arm affectionately.

They were interrupted by a sharp knock on the back door which announced the entrance of Jean Evans, their neighbour. "Sorry but I couldn't wait a moment longer to meet Joe's young lady."

"Come in, Jean, you know you're always welcome. Why, you're almost one of the family."

Joe and Eva jumped up from where they had been sitting beside the square table. "I'm very pleased to meet you Mrs. Evans," said Eva shyly.

"I must say Joe, she really is as pretty as you said. He never shuts up about you. It's Eva this and Eva that all day long."

Eva found she could not help but smile at this diminutive woman who seemed to have an abundance of energy and who had not stood still since she entered the room.

"And you must be Eva's Mam and Dad," Jean continued, shaking hands with Thomas and Bella. "You mustn't worry about her, she will be quite comfortable, you know. Ginny will keep both of them warm as toast, I'm sure." A ripple of laughter ran round the room.

Thomas rose from his chair and cleared his throat. "Hrrm we brought you a little something to see you over the holidays," he said, passing over the Christmas hamper.

"There was no need, you know, but I won't say I am not grateful for a little extra, so I will accept it in the manner it was given. Thank you very much." Her head bobbing up and down in agreement.

Bella was highly amused by this and struggled to keep a straight face. "I'm sure you're more than welcome, Mrs. Evans. We are all so glad Joe has found himself such a wonderful landlady."

Blushing, for once Jean Evans seemed lost for words, "I'm sure it's what any Christian woman would do Mrs. Greenall."

"Please, call me Bella, and this is my husband, Tom."

Jean acknowledged this introduction with another bob of her head. "I'll be off now Ellen, but just give me a knock on the fireback if you want anything."

Eva looked a little puzzled until Ginny explained that in colliery communities it was standard practice to knock sharply on the metal plate at the back of the fire grate with a poker if you needed help. This was especially true when the woman next door was pregnant, like Ellen, and may need immediate assistance when alone in the house.

Ellen crossed the room and laid her hand gently on the older woman's arm. "We would like it very much if you would join us for Christmas dinner on Tuesday, Jean. That's if you have nothing else planned, of course. I know it might be a bit of a squash but there's always room for one more good friend."

"That is very kind of you. I will be attending Morning Service but I must say I wasn't looking forward to spending the rest of the day alone. I always miss my Bob most at Christmas; it's certainly a time for families not for lonely old biddies like me."

"You're certainly no old biddy," Joe laughed, "but

you are welcome to be a part of our family for as long as you like." And he wrapped his great arms around the little woman and lifted her clean off the floor.

"Get off you daft ha'peth," Jean protested, pushing futilely against his huge shoulders. "Let me down so's I can go and straighten your room ready for the ladies' visit."

As soon as Joe lessened his hold, Jean flitted away through the back door, calling her goodbyes as she went.

"I guess we should be making tracks too, Bella. I don't like the look of those clouds; we might get some snow before the days out I'm thinking."

Bella rose, tears filling her eyes as she turned to say goodbye to Eva. "It'll be a quiet Christmas without you, love," she said squeezing Eva's hands between her own, "but I'm sure you'll have a wonderful time here, with Joe. You both have a lot of catching up to do."

Eva, too, was very close to tears as she gave first her mother and then her father a final hug. "It's only for a few days, Mam, then Dad'll be back to collect us on Boxing Day. You could probably both do with a good rest before the shop opens again on Thursday. And remember to open your presents; I left them under the tree."

Thomas said goodbye to Ellen, Jack and Ginny, then turned and shook hands with Joe. "Have a grand Christmas lad and take care of that lass of mine." A knowing look passed between them; they understood each other perfectly.

"Don't bother to come out," Bella halted Ginny as she rose to follow them outside. "It's perishing out there. Have a lovely Christmas and I'll be along to see you when you're back home." To Ginny's surprise, Bella leant over and kissed her warmly on the cheek.

Joe insisted on accompanying them to their car, however, and once Bella was settled in the front passenger seat, a tartan blanket snugly over her knees, he and Thomas spent a minute or two in earnest conversation before Thomas finally climbed into the driver's seat and they set off up the street.

On the drive home, Thomas remained silent. It would be the first time Eva had ventured forth without them but they had the reassurance that she was in safe hands. "I think Eva could do much worse than Joe Fishburn, Tom, what do you think?"

"He's a good lad, right enough, from good stock. At the end of the day, I don't think it'll be up to us, Bel; our Eva always had a mind of her own and I wouldn't have it any other way."

Bella smiled to herself reassured that her husband had at last become reconciled to Eva and Joe's relationship. With wedding bells ringing in her mind, she looked out of the window to what might lie ahead. Who knew what 1924 might bring.

CHAPTER SEVENTEEN

Despite the lowering skies, the snow held off. After enjoying a huge Sunday's dinner consisting of roast beef, three vegetables and fluffy Yorkshire puddings (courtesy of Ginny's magic touch), Joe and Eva decided it would be worth facing the bitter cold to get out of the house for an hour or so. Wrapping themselves up warmly, they set off for a walk along the beach banks, passing by the colliery gates on the way.

"It looks much bigger than the pits round our way," Eva commented, gazing in awe at the huge pit wheels, stilled now for the holidays. "Does it close down completely for Christmas, then?"

"There's no coal produced," Joe answered, "but there will still be teams of men carrying out necessary maintenance work, even on Christmas Day." In fact, even though he would have welcomed the extra money, Joe had turned down the chance to work overtime during the shutdown, Joe wanted to spend every minute he could with Eva. "And, of course, the ponies always need looking after."

Passing by an assortment of allotment gardens, Joe took Eva's hand to gently guide her over the worst of the puddles and pot holes that riddled the rough pathways. It was a good job she had decided to wear her galoshes, Eva thought.

They continued under the railway bridge towards the cliff tops. Coal was transported in huge trucks via the railway to the coke ovens at Hawdene, to the docks at Seaham and to the iron and steel works at Hartlepool. To the right a track ran parallel to the railway lines, while ahead of them stretched a well-worn path alongside a deep dene. Far below, Eva could see a beck burbling along towards the sea, despite being frozen over in places. The sides of the dene were covered with trees and shrubs, most divested of their leaves for the Winter so that they stood out like skeletons against the tangle of undergrowth. Several paths lead downwards, obviously made by some animal or another, or perhaps even by small boys intent on adventure.

As they came to the mouth of the dene the North Sea lay before them. Eva thought it frightening and inhospitable; great waves rolled over the expanse of steel grey water; gulls screamed as they swooped and dived again and again into the depths, intent on catching the gleaming silver fish that darted below the surface.

Cautiously, they made their way down the steep cliff path until they reached the safety of the beach below. Parts of the cliffs had fallen away, strewing the sand with giant rocks and boulders. Deep caverns ate into the cliff, eroded by fierce winter tides. The swollen stream broke into rivulets as it exited the dene, seeking to mate once again with the salt water.

Along the water's edge several fishermen stood like solitary sentinels, rods held aloft above the frothing waves, watching, waiting for the tell-tale knock on the tip to signal an unwary fish ready to take the worm on the hook. Speed and strength of the hunter pitted against a prey fighting for its life, as the fisherman struck into the fish, wedging the hook solidly into its mouth; the long, tortuous struggle to bring it in; reel turning continuously until the fish was landed and dispatched quickly by a single blow to the back of its head. This was no sport, Eva realised, but a matter of survival; a single cod enough to feed an entire family.

They said little; the roar of the breakers on the sand and the shrill whistling wind sharp in their ears made talking difficult. But they did not care, content in their own company. Hand in hand, they crunched their way over the strand towards a row of ramshackle huts, used by the miners to house their sturdy cobble boats.

Joe stopped beside the third hut; its wooden boards

thickly tarred against the salt air; taking a key from his pocket, he unlocked the door and stepped aside so Eva could enter. Warmth from a small coal stove in the corner welcomed them. Eva realised they were in a small room partitioned off from the rest of the boathouse. Although the entire room was makeshift it was nevertheless comfortable. An old horsehair sofa took up most of one wall, with cushions in faded pinks and greens. Wintry light struggled to penetrate threadbare sheeting, hung at the window as a curtain. A wooden stool could serve as an extra seat or a small table depending on need.

"Sit yourself down love, and I'll see about getting the kettle on. I daresay a cup of hot tea wouldn't come amiss." Joe filled the kettle with water from a bottle he had carried in his pocket, then set it to boil on top of the stove. Meanwhile, he retrieved a teapot and two cups from a shelf on the wall opposite, adding a spoon of tea to the pot from the caddy also housed there. "I'm afraid there's no milk so we'll have to have it black but at least it'll be warm and wet."

"Joe, where are we? Who does this hut belong to?"

"Fred, one of the blokes I work with. He calls it his Riviera Retreat. This is where he comes when he wants to get away from his Missus for a few hours.

Him and his pal have a small boat but he doesn't go out fishing very often. Still, he doesn't tell his wife that and his mate makes sure he gets enough fish to keep her happy."

Eva smiled as she tried to imagine what this Fred must be like. She was glad that Joe seemed to be making friends so quickly but aware that he now had a new life in which she played no part.

"His mate was out this morning setting his lobster pots, so he built up the stove to last 'til we got here and Fred lent me his key."

Flattered that Joe had gone to so much trouble for her, Eva could not resist the opportunity to tease him. "And I suppose you did all this just to get me alone and to have your wicked way with me." She tried to look horrified, but Joe was having none of it.

"Of course, what else?" He pulled her to him, holding her hands behind her back so she was helpless to resist him as he kissed her deeply. There was no resistance, only willingness as Eva matched his passion with her own, her heart racing, her colour rising, a low moan escaping her lips. Joe buried his face in her hair, drinking in the unique smell of her. "I've missed you so much. I thought my heart might burst for the wanting of you."

Drawing back, Eva gazed into his eyes, almost black now with desire. "I've thought about you every minute of every day. I dream of you every night." She blushed now even to think of some of those dreams. If he had pressed her then to lie with him, here in this simple fisherman's hut, she would have so that she could carry that memory home, to sustain her.

He saw it there in her eyes, but he was stronger than that, and he put her from him then so that the spell was broken and his respect for her remained intact.

Slowly, Joe guided her back to sit on the sofa while he finished making the tea. Time was short; it would soon be dark and it was too dangerous to try to negotiate the cliff path without torch or even moonlight to aid them.

They talked about all they had done since they parted three weeks before. Eva told him about the children's antics in school and how proud she had been when they had performed their Nativity Play. Joe told her about Stan and Fred, his new marras; how they had made him feel welcome and how they watched out for each other.

But he didn't tell her about the dangers he faced every day; how the roof could give way with little notice; how the salt water seeped into your very bones, causing collars to rub the skin off your neck;

how the gas could creep up on you unawares sending you to sleep forever.

Back in Bourne Street, Ginny and Ellen sat in peace, either side of the fire. They too were drinking tea. Jack had taken Alice upstairs for her nap. He loved to sit watching over her as she slept, and it would give the women some time to themselves to catch up and put the world to rights.

"Whoever would have thought our Joe and Eva Greenall?" Ellen said.

"And why ever not?" Ginny replied rather sharply.

"Well the Greenall's are a bit well to do, Ginny."

"I think you are forgetting Tom Greenall grew up in the same road as we did, and his dad was a right wrongun."

"I know that, but Bella's folks are really well off, aren't they?" Ellen knew she was on dodgy ground as far as Ginny was concerned.

"That's as may be, but Bella Greenall's got no side to her. She thinks the world of our Joe and knows he will make Eva a good husband. She'll want for nowt as long as he has breath in his body."

"Now Ginny, settle down, there's no need to get so worked up. I think Eva's a lovely lass and she's a good match for our Joe. She'll certainly keeps him on his toes. I wonder where they've got to; it's starting to get dark and it's perishing out there."

Ellen rose from her chair to draw the curtains against the night chill, taking the chance to peer down the street to see if there was any sign of the couple. Her hand automatically strayed to rub her swollen abdomen.

"By I think this must be a boy; he's got a good kick that's for sure. Mebbe he'll play for England one day."

Jack appeared at the foot of the stairs carrying Alice on his shoulders. Stooping to pass under the doorway, he smiled at his wife. "Well let's hope he'll be the first of many. We could have our own football team one day!"

"I don't think so, not unless men suddenly start having babies then you can produce half the team yourself." An icy blast swept through from the kitchen as Joe and Eva rushed in through the back door. Discarding their shoes and hanging their coats in the cupboard under the stairs, they crossed to warm their hands by the fire.

"It's coming on to snow again, I think," Joe said.

He turned to Eva and continued, "With a bit of luck it'll snow heavy all over Christmas and you will have to stay until it thaws."

"Dream on," Ginny said, "by the radio it's supposed to turn milder. We'll be lucky to see a white Christmas this year. Joe, you can help carry our things into next door, then I'll be back to give a hand with the tea. C'mon Eva, look sharp, or Jean will be wondering where we've got to."

CHAPTER EIGHTEEN

Christmas Day Eva woke early. It was still pitch-black outside, not even the birds were up yet. Ginny snored gently beside her. Jean had been right about Ginny keeping her warm; it was like snuggling up to a giant hot water bottle covered in flannelette.

Eva lay as still as she could manage. She knew that Ginny was up before dawn every day back home; she deserved a bit of a lie-in on Christmas Day. It was going to be a wonderful Christmas. She hoped everyone would like the presents she'd brought. Not for the first time she wondered what Joe had got her. They had agreed not to spend much because they needed to save up for when they got married. He might think the cufflinks she had bought him a little extravagant but he could wear them on their Wedding Day.

At last there were signs that Jean was up and about. Familiar sounds rose such as the fire grate being raked out to stir new life into the dying embers; the water singing through the pipes as the kettle was filled for the first pot of the day; dishes and cups being lifted from the cupboard to lay the breakfast table.

Ginny stirred. "Merry Christmas lass."

"A very merry Christmas to you too, Ginny. Do you think Joe will be up yet?"

"I dare say he will but let's at least have a bite of breakfast before we land on Ellen's doorstep; give her a chance to get squared round."

Although her face fell a little, Eva could offer no reasonable argument against Ginny's logic, but that did not stop her climbing unceremoniously over the top of the older woman, gasping as her bare feet landed on the cold linoleum floor. Quickly finding her slippers, she pulled on her quilted dressing gown.

Drawing back the curtains, she breathed a sigh of relief. "At least there's been no snow through the night. A white Christmas is very romantic, but it's no fun running across the yard to the toilet through six inches of snow."

Ginny smiled. "Get yourself downstairs and let me get me clothes on in peace. Jean's up so there'll be a nice cup of tea on the go."

After breakfast Eva helped clear the table and wash-up the dishes. She was too excited to sit still and tried to hurry the others along. They seemed to be deliberately finding things to do slowing down any progress.

"Do you think we need a coat, Ginny," Jean enquired, "or will we get away with our cardigans?"

"We're only going next-door not to the North Pole," Eva spluttered. "Let's go or they'll think we're not coming."

The two older women made a show of gathering their things, then at last they were ready, leaving the house by the back door. Eva still found it hard to believe that no-one ever locked their doors if they were not going far but as Jean said, it was not as if they had much worth stealing. And in such a close-knit community most valued their honesty.

Even though they were expected, Ginny still knocked before entering her sister's house. They were greeted by a very excited Alice, "Smelly Kissmas Aunty Ginny!" She raised her arms to be lifted so that she could plant a resounding kiss on her aunt's cheek.

"Merry Christmas to you too, young lady." Ginny swung her niece around before settling her onto her hip. "Were you a good girl this year? Did Santa fill your stocking with presents or did he leave you a bag of ashes for being naughty?"

Alice wriggled free, took her aunt's hand and guided her to the stocking which now lay on the hearthrug before the fire. Ginny, pausing long enough to wish all a Merry Christmas, made a great fuss as the little girl took each item from her stocking. A rag doll poked its head over the top; beneath this were a ball, an apple and an orange, a few nuts and a silver sixpence. Alice was obviously delighted.

Joe and Eva sat together holding hands on the sofa under the window. "Can I give Alice her present now," Eva asked, "or do you want me to wait until after dinner?"

"Give it to her now. With any luck, she'll go down for a sleep after dinner; we can do grown-up presents then."

Eva had wrapped the whip and spinning top in Christmas paper with pictures of Santa in his sleigh on it. Alice accepted it rather shyly then took it to her mother to help her unwrap it carefully, obviously not wanting to tear the pretty paper. Her eyes lit up when she saw what was inside.

"Oooh t'ank you, t'ank you, Eva," she cried, then carried the toy to her father so that he could show her how to make it spin.

"You're very welcome, angel," Eva replied, squeezing Joe's hand tightly, delighted with the little girl's response.

The Christmas dinner was truly a feast fit for kings. A succulent roast goose took pride of place, a dish of sage and onion stuffing ready at its side. Soon every plate was piled high with roasted potatoes and parsnips, carrots and swede together with a generous helping of Brussels sprouts. Tasty onion gravy, almost thick enough to stand your spoon up in, completed the meal.

Thomas and Bella had thoughtfully supplied drinks: wine for the ladies and beer for the men. But perhaps the best accompaniment of all was the generous supply of laughter and good spirits that emanated from family and friends seated at the table.

Clearing the plates, Ginny emerged proudly from the scullery bearing an enormous Plum Pudding, topped with flaming brandy. Although everyone protested they lacked room for one more mouthful, no-one could resist a small portion of this fine dessert, helped on its way by smooth vanilla custard.

Once the dishes had all been sided away to be washed later just this once, everyone retrieved the presents they had brought from under the Christmas tree. None of these had cost the giver very much money but it was obvious that they had all put a great deal of thought into their selection.

Ginny loved her new leather gloves, declaring their appearance timely as her old ones were quite shabby, fit only for gardening now. Ellen received a pretty Paisley shawl, blue to match her eyes. Jack was so content with his new briar pipe that he set to at once to burn out the bowl to make it fit for his after-dinner smoke.

Joe, as Eva predicted, protested the expense of his silver cufflinks, saying no-one had ever given him a more handsome present.

Eva could hardly contain her own excitement as she waited her turn. Joe held out what seemed to be a square box wrapped in golden paper and tied with fine velvet ribbon. Slowly she undid the delicate binding before carefully unwrapping the paper, folding it and setting it to one side. Inside, lay a box which had quite obviously once contained chocolates or some such confection.

Everyone held their breath as she finally lifted the lid to reveal several layers of tissue paper. Gently parting this, she revealed her present: the fern fossil Joe had found on his first day down the new pit. He had polished it until it shone, the fern now black as ebony contrasting against the grey of the stone that held it.

"It's beautiful, Joe," Eva said, her eyes bright with tears. "Wherever did you find it?"

Joe recounted how he had found the fossil and its true origins, and how he had spent many hours polishing it until it shone. Eva was touched at the amount of love that had gone into her remarkable gift.

"It will look lovely on my school desk as a paperweight," she said, "and I can tell the children all about it. Then they can run home and get into lots of trouble raking around their coal houses looking for more examples." Once again laughter rang out amongst the company.

Presents opened and dishes at last washed, the two older ladies retired back to Jean's, possibly for a late afternoon snooze. Ellen, feeling the strain of the morning, also went upstairs for a lie down before Alice woke. Jack took himself off to see to his garden, for no matter what, the hens needed feeding and the eggs collecting.

Joe and Eva made the most of their solitude, sitting sociably together on the sofa, contentment spreading over them. Joe slipped his arm around Eva's shoulder and drew her to him.

"Eva," he began, "I know we haven't been courting very long, but you do know that I love you very much, don't you?"

Eva's heart began to beat faster as she tried to second guess what Joe's next move might be. "And I love you too, Joe, with all my heart," she almost whispered, turning her face to be kissed.

Instead, Joe leapt up off the sofa and began to pace in front of the fire. "I know I don't have much to offer you yet," he continued, "and you could probably do much better."

"Where was this going?" Eva wondered.

Suddenly Joe went down on one knee before her and took a small ring case from his pocket, opened it and offered it to her. "Eva, my love, will you marry me?"

Eva gulped. What would her father say?

"Oh yes Joe, of course I'll marry you," and she leant forward and kissed him. Drawing back, she continued, "But perhaps we had better keep it to ourselves for now."

Joe knew exactly what she was thinking and sought to put her mind at rest. "It's alright, Eva, I've already asked your dad if he would have any objections and surprisingly he thought it would be a good idea, so long as we wait and save so that we can afford to set up home properly."

He took the ring from its box and slipped it onto her finger. The single diamond caught the light from the fire, sending rainbow reflections across the ceiling.

"But how …?" She was at a loss to know how he could afford such an obviously expensive ring.

"Ginny." He said simply and went on to explain how Ginny had given them her own engagement ring and the story of Edwin.

Eva was stunned. The beauty of the solitaire which now adorned her hand; the love which shone from Joe's eyes and her father who really did seem to have had a change of heart; doubtless her mother had had something to do with that. This might just turn out to be the best Christmas ever.

CHAPTER NINETEEN

Winter dragged on. Icy winds drove everyone indoors; snow often covered the fields. January and February were long and cold with rain making everyone's life a misery. When the weather allowed, Joe cycled over on Sundays to meet Eva. Once or twice her father took Eva across to Essingham, spending an afternoon with Ginny and Ellen while she visited with Joe before driving her home again.

It seemed to Joe that he hardly ever saw daylight so that it became hard to distinguish between time spent down the pit or on the surface. Even during the day, constant cloud cover hid the sun turning the world to grey.

Eva shivered in her classroom despite the stove that burnt in the corner which was invariably shrouded by mittens and hats put there by the children to dry. Although March was a little drier, the cold remained relentless. Scarves and gloves remained the order of the day. Evenings were spent in front of the fire listening to the radio.

In February, Ellen was safely delivered of a bouncing baby boy, who they named James after Jack's father. At a healthy eight pounds, he was already making his presence felt in the household, especially around four in the morning. Alice was besotted with him, insisted on helping to bathe him and even changing his nappies whenever she was given the chance. He spent most of the day in his perambulator, which took up an inordinate amount of space in their living room. At night, he slept snugly between his parents in their double bed, until he rose before the cockerels to give them an early morning call.

Although April started poorly, by Easter the weather turned warm and sunny. Days were becoming longer so Joe often cycled to Wain Hill on Saturday night so that he and Eva had most of Sunday together.

They began to make plans for their future and refused to be disheartened by the long-term nature of their ambitions. Even if they were wed, Joe could not put his name down on the waiting list for a colliery house until after he was married. They seemed to be trapped in a vicious circle. Until, that is, Jean Evans came up with a possible solution.

If they didn't mind living in somewhat cramped conditions, she was willing to let them move in with her until they could be allocated a house of their own. Eva could spend much of her day next door; she was certain Ellen would be glad of an extra pair of hands.

Joe finished work at six o'clock on Saturday morning and by eight he was cycling for all he was worth to give Eva the good news. She was delighted. At last they could be together. If it had been up to Joe and Eva they would have booked their date at the Registry Office immediately but Eva knew her mother and father would not stand for that. However, her father's reaction once again surprised her.

All that winter, Thomas had had to listen to Bella and Eva making wedding plans. He knew they had already sorted out the details of where and when and even who was to be invited. The main stumbling block was Joe. Weddings did not come cheap and while it was the responsibility of the bride's father to pay for most of the wedding, Joe was a proud man and would not take kindly to what he might see as charity.

While the women might think they had things sorted, Tom had one or two plans of his own. If the wedding took place here in Wain Hill then the groom's costs such as the cars and the wedding breakfast venue could be kept to a minimum. His own position as Church Warden and his business connections as a grocer should also help. A summer wedding would suit all round. He'd even taken

Eva's employment into account as she would not be allowed to continue teaching once she married. It would be more convenient, therefore, if she left at the end of the school year when they broke up for the summer holidays.

Once again, he was standing in front of the fireplace in the sitting room; his customary position when he thought he had something important to say. Bella sat quietly for once, a little worried how her husband was going to react to the proposition.

"Well," he began clearing his throat before continuing. He was obviously quite enjoying holding them in thrall. "I can find no objection to you two getting married, but.."

All three held their breath.

"I definitely think you should not dilly dally. You are obviously very much in love and I don't think I can stand Eva mooning around the house for much longer." And he set out his own proposals at the end of which there was an audible release of breath before everyone started talking at once.

Roland was dispatched to fetch Ginny and once again the plans were laid out before her. Champagne was poured to toast the happy couple and laughter rang out well into the night. By the next morning everything was settled. Now all they had to do was book the church and the hall, arrange for the banns to be read, agree on a menu for the wedding breakfast, order flowers, hire a Bridal car, decide on bridesmaids, page boys, groomsmen and best man, find a wedding dress, order a new suit for Joe, make certain no one's outfits clashed and all before August. What could be simpler?

Thomas took Joe aside and insisted he allow him to take care of their honeymoon. By the end of the weekend, Joe's head was buzzing with details. Of course, he was happy but he was also worried what all this would cost but he was determined that he would pay his way. The new pit was crying out for men to volunteer for overtime. He and Eva may not see much of each other before the wedding.

CHAPTER TWENTY

Joe stretched out on his old bed, head resting comfortably on the familiar pillow, feet almost touching the footboard. Being July, the sun had already been up for hours and he could hear Ginny as she went about her morning chores. Wedding Day or no Wedding Day the animals still needed tending then turning out into fields and pens for the day.

He listened as Ginny stirred life back into the fire, filled the kettle and settled it onto the coals to boil. The smell of frying bacon drove him from his bed, empty belly rumbling despite his nerves. He pulled on trousers and an old shirt, found his shoes where he had kicked them off the night before and headed downstairs to the kitchen. From today it would be his wife who would greet him every morning not his sister.

"Morning sunshine," Ginny greeted him, "wondered when you were going to show. Sit yourself down and I'll pour your tea."

Joe gave her a lop-sided grin as he pulled a chair out at the table and sat down. She smiled as she watched him tuck into his plate of bacon, eggs, tomatoes and fried bread with the energy of the working man. "I hope Eva can cook half as good as you, Sis," he spluttered between mouthfuls. "It's hungry work down that pit."

"She'll learn same as the rest of us, I dare say. I'm sure our Ellen and Jean will give out plenty of advice," she chuckled as she went out into the yard to fetch the tin bath off the wall. Setting it in front of the fire she began to fill it with buckets of cold water from the scullery before adding steaming water from the set pot. "I'm going upstairs to get ready. Mind you don't take too long lying dreaming in this bath; there's still plenty to see to before we go off to church."

Things were by no means so tranquil in the Greenall household that morning. Thomas managed to escape to the bottom of the garden, hiding himself surreptitiously behind the chestnut tree before lighting up a cigarette to calm his nerves. Bella did not like him smoking and had forbidden it in the house but she would be far too busy to notice his absence amid the mayhem that seemed to have overtaken his home.

Eva sat before her dressing table mirror wearing nothing but a sheer silk chemise, her wedding gown suspended from the wardrobe door awaiting the right moment. Her mother had shooed everyone else from the room wanting a few quiet moments alone with her daughter before the excitement of the day overwhelmed them. Lucy, relishing her role as Chief Bridesmaid, had been dispatched to look after the two younger bridesmaids and page boy.

Bella picked up a hairbrush and began brushing Eva's short bob until it shone. Eva closed her eyes allowing the rhythmic strokes to soothe her.

"Happy?" Bella enquired. Eva nodded, a satisfied smile playing on her lips. How could she be anything other than happy? Today she and Joe would become one and tonight, at last, the months of waiting would be over.

Struggling to broach such a delicate subject, Bella clasped Eva's shoulders, looking into the eyes of her reflection. "Is there anything you want to ask me, about, well you know? Only some girl's might find their first time rather frightening."

Eva swivelled on her stool until she faced her mother. "I must confess I am a little frightened," she began, "but I know Joe would never do anything to hurt me," blushing she continued, "so I have to admit I'm feeling rather excited too. Is that wrong of me, Mam?"

"No child, when two people truly love each other, the marital bed can be the happiest place in the world." Nevertheless, she offered up a silent prayer that her future son-in-law would prove to be as gentle and generous a lover as her husband had always been.

Eva rose and went into her mother's arms and hugged her tightly. Bella blinked away her tears as she pulled away. "Right, young lady let's get Lucy in here and get you into your dress." Then she left to call her daughter's best friend from the top of the stairs.

Eva turned and gazed at herself in the cheval mirror. Today everything would change forever. Little Eva Greenall would be replaced by Mrs. Joseph Fishburn and an innocent young girl would become a woman. She shivered, not with fear, but with anticipation.

Downstairs in the lounge, Thomas paced nervously. Now dressed in his sombre three-piece suit, he checked his tie in the mirror above the mantel. If it had been up to him they would have had full morning dress but Eva had put her foot down on it. For the tenth time, he retrieved his speech from his inside jacket pocket, put on his spectacles, and appraised the words written there; he did not know how he was going to get through it without breaking down. Of course, he was happy, Eva and Joe were so obviously suited, and he trusted Joe to make a good husband but he did not feel ready to give his only daughter into the keeping of another. Crossing to the sideboard, he poured himself another stiff whiskey. It would have to be his last; it would not do for Thomas Greenall, father of the bride, pillar of the community, to turn up tipsy to his daughter's wedding.

Bella, resplendent in a pale blue costume with matching hat, entered the room and came to stand beside him, laying her hand gently on his arm. She could smell the whiskey on his breath but satisfied herself with a sharp look rather than berating him for his drinking.

Eva stood framed in the doorway, so beautiful he found it hard to speak. She seemed to glow with happiness: her ankle-length dress of lace over silk, had a fashionable dropped waist; a long veil flowed down from a crowning cloche trimmed with flowers. In her hands she carried a bouquet of pink roses and lily-of-the-valley. A pair of heeled white satin slippers completed the outfit.

"I'd better get going. Lucy and the little ones are already in the car." She crossed to Eva, taking her hands and squeezed them tightly. "The next time we meet you will be Mrs. Joe Fishburn." Turning to her husband she said, "The Bridal car won't be long. See you in church."

Eva crossed to her father. "Well Dad, will I do?"

Thomas cleared his throat loudly. "You look beautiful; you remind me of your mother on our Wedding Day." He placed his hand under her chin and tilted her face up so he could look into her eyes. He did not have to ask if she was happy. "Remember, if ever you need us we will always be here."

She reached up to hug him tightly, arms about his neck, just as she had when she was a little girl. "Now, now, you'll get yourself in a mess and your Mother will go mad." A car horn beeped twice. "We'd better be off although I will get the driver to go twice round the village. I understand it is customary for the bride to be a little late and it will do that young man of yours good to be kept waiting for once."

As they emerged from the front door, they were greeted by a crowd of well-wishers: a few neighbours and many customers who were hoping to catch a glimpse of the bride. To one side, Eva was delighted to see many of the pupils she had taught. Bristling with pride, Thomas handed her safely into the car before turning and throwing a large handful of coins into the air. The children shouted, "Shabby Weddings!" before diving to retrieve the expected bounty.

CHAPTER TWENTY-ONE

Joe waited nervously at the front of the church. Jack, a true friend now, stood as his Best Man, looking every bit as anxious. Behind them the church was filled to bursting. Relatives lined the pews: Eva's family to the left, Joe's to the right. Muffled chatter and laughter rose amongst their friends who lined the rear rows. The Reverend Shepherd waited patiently in front of the altar, smiling acknowledgement to Bella as she took her place beside her son, Roland in the first pew.

It seemed to Joe as if the old church was holding its breath in anticipation of the solemn ceremony to come. It was warm, even for July. Scent from the exquisite floral decorations either side of the nave hung heavy in the air. Joe ran his finger nervously around his starched white collar. Glancing sideways at Jack, his friend gave him a reassuring nod.

Suddenly, the congregation stilled as the organist struck up the opening chords of 'Here Comes the Bride'. Joe turned to look at his bride; she almost took his breath away. Eva, an angel in purest white, proceeded on her father's arm; while Thomas could not have looked prouder or more dignified. The two pretty Flower girls preceded them, strewing the aisle with blossom from their baskets. The pageboy, smart as a pin in his satin sailor suit, walked behind holding the short train safely off the ground. Lastly, elegant in a soft pink gown, carrying a bouquet of white carnations, came Lucy, keeping a careful eye on her young charges.

"How handsome Joe looks," thought Eva, "and how happy." She glided slowly down the central aisle, her eyes never leaving his until at last she arrived at his side, where her father gave her up into his keeping and retreated to stand beside Bella.

"Dearly beloved..." the ceremony began, though how much the young couple were aware of the solemnity of the vows they were undertaking was debatable. Eva held her breath as Joe slipped the simple gold band onto her finger, a symbol of their unity. "You may kiss the bride." Their lips met in a kiss of infinite tenderness, and then it was over. They were now man and wife.

The sun shone gloriously as the wedding party met on the steps to have the obligatory photographs taken. Many relatives took the opportunity to catch up with distant cousins as they waited for their turn before the camera. Children were admonished to stand still and stop wriggling; all they longed for was the freedom to play tag amongst the gravestones. At last the photographer was satisfied that he had recorded every guest for posterity and everyone was given leave to proceed to the Welfare Hall for the Wedding Reception.

The hundred or so guests milled about in the ante-room, helping themselves to drinks from the bar until the bride and groom stood ready to receive them. The Welfare Hall, though not the most romantic of venues, looked resplendent: crystal glasses sparkled against pristine white tablecloths; silver cutlery shined to a mirror finish. The sun shone through the high windows bathing the tableaux in golden light.

One by one the guests were greeted by Joe and Eva before moving on to find their seats at one of the tables in the large hall. Only when every last guest was in, did the pair take their places at the high table in front of the stage. To one side sat Thomas and Ginny, while Bella and Roland sat at the other. A fine Wedding Cake stood on the table immediately in front of the pair. Three tiers high, the white icing was smooth as glass and was decorated with swags and intricate medallions. On the top stood a miniature Bride and Groom. Ginny sat proud as punch of her handiwork; it had been her gift to her brother and his new bride. Thomas stood to say Grace, then a procession of waitresses began to serve the food. Thomas beamed; his wealth of contacts within the food trade had certainly come in handy.

Waldorf Salad, with fresh rolls and butter, was quickly followed by succulent Loin of Lamb, stuffed with Rosemary and Garlic pate, served on a bed of Herb Mashed Potato, with Honey Roasted Vegetables and Red Currant Sauce. There was red wine for the grown-ups and fresh orange juice for the children. The dessert course was Chocolate Tart served with Crushed Strawberry Compote, the lusciousness of which was evidenced on every young child's face. Everyone agreed that it was a feast fit for kings.

Once the tables were cleared of plates, everyone was given a glass of champagne with which to toast the happy couple. Speeches were made. Thomas almost breaking down, Jack adding humour to the occasion with a joke or two; Joe thanking everyone for coming, finally turning to Eva and once again promising to do everything within his power to make her half as happy as she had made him that day.

Speeches over, the tables were moved from the centre of the room to make way for a dance floor. The same band that had played in the Church Hall for their first dance together had been hired again; it had seemed fitting somehow. The bride and groom took to the floor for the first waltz to the strains of, 'If you were the only girl in the world.' Everyone clapped and cheered as they completed a full circuit, then quickly joined them. Thomas and Bella glided effortlessly around the room, while Roland, gallant as ever, swooped up Lucy and guided her expertly through the first of many dances. Even Ginny, who tried to insist she couldn't dance, was pulled to her feet by Jimmy Bell, who seemed to scrub up quite nicely given half a chance. A grand air of bonhomie pervaded the room, assisted no doubt by the copious amounts of alcohol flowing freely from the bar. Thomas Greenall had certainly done his daughter and her new husband proud.

All too soon, it was time for the newlyweds to leave the festivities, although those left behind would party on without them. Joe and Eva slipped into an ante-room to change into their going-away outfits then returned to the hall to say their final goodbyes. Roland was to drive them to Durham Station in his father's car which was now suitably bedecked with the requisite tails of tin cans and old boots and displayed a 'Just Married' placard in the rear window.

Thomas and Bella, Ginny, Jack and Ellen followed them out to wave them off. Only now did Thomas take an envelope out of his pocket and hand it to Joe. Inside were two return train tickets for Scarborough. "A car will be waiting for you at Scarborough Station to take you on to your final destination. Have a wonderful time and one of us will meet you at this end on your return."

No amount of protestation would persuade him to reveal where they would be staying but by the smug expression on his face and the width of the smile on Bella's, it promised to be somewhere special. One final round of kisses, then they were off. As soon as the car disappeared from view, Ginny turned to Thomas. "Just where have you sent them, Tom?" she asked.

"Why, to The Grand Hotel of course. Only the best for my family."

CHAPTER TWENTY-TWO

The green locomotive thundered into Durham Station amid great clouds of steam. Joe and Eva made their way down the platform, boarded the second of the brown coaches, and found their allocated seats in a compartment halfway down the corridor. They were delighted to find they were the only occupants. Joe easily lifted their cases onto the luggage rack above their heads before taking his seat by the window opposite Eva. He did not trust himself to sit beside her for fear of losing all control; who knew who might come in. Holding hands, they kept up a steady stream of conversation until they heard the announcement for changes at York.

Their second train to Scarborough was modern compared to the first and had open carriages that reminded them of one of the 'buses they were more used to travelling on. Eva slipped her arm through Joe's as they sat side by side, every so often gazing down at the new wedding ring that nestled on the third finger of her left hand as if she still couldn't believe it was there. Together they gazed over the vastness of the open moors as they sped through making their way to the coast.

With a whoosh of steam and a squeal of brakes they

pulled into Scarborough Station. Alighting onto the platform, they took in the splendour of the glass roof supported by an intricate structure of iron girders, before following the steady stream of passengers making for the exit. Passing under the square entrance tower, complete with clock and cupula, they were approached by an extremely smart chauffeur. "Mr. and Mrs. Joseph Fishburn?" he enquired. They nodded. "I've been sent by The Grand Hotel to collect you. If you'd like to follow me, please." He relieved them of their luggage and lead the way to a shining limousine that was parked nearby.

Joe and Eva found difficulty in keeping straight faces as the chauffeur held the rear door open for them. Once inside, they both tried to talk at once, filled with excitement and wonder. Everyone had heard of The Grand Hotel, of course, once the biggest and finest hotel in Europe, but never in their wildest dreams did they think they would ever be guests there. Only for a moment did Joe allow a shadow to cross his face as he thought of what it must have cost Eva's father but decided to accept this gift in the spirit it was surely given; he would make sure that his concerns did not spoil Eva's enjoyment. He only hoped they would not incur too many incidental expenses.

Approaching the hotel from the North, they had an

excellent view of the V-shape of its construction, a tribute to the late Queen Victoria. Pulling up at the front of the building, they could only gaze in amazement; it certainly lived up to its name. Floor after floor of rooms rose before them: white bricks carried ornamental moulded red brick jambs, while cornices were picked out in rich Yorkshire stone. The main entrance consisted of an ornate Romanesque arch, supported by rose-coloured Italian marble pillars. The chauffeur retrieved their cases, as a liveried doorman came down the steps to greet them. "Welcome to The Grand Hotel, Sir, Madam. If you would follow me, please, I will show you to reception where you can check in."

If they thought the façade of the hotel was impressive, then the opulence of the main hall took their breath away. In the centre stood an enormous jardinière filled with exotic plants. This stood beneath a huge dome which did much to keep the air cool on even the hottest days. Surrounding the hall, tall, stately arches gave access to various salons, but even these were eclipsed by the grandeur of the main staircase, a wide sweep of steps leading to a balcony on the floor above, which ran around the full perimeter. In the hall below, fashionable society milled about or sat on comfortable chairs at one of the many occasional tables.

Eva held tightly onto Joe's arm as they made their

way towards the main reception desk, a rather more discrete station in one corner of the hall. The receptionist checked their names against his register then gave their room keys to the bellboy who stood by their luggage. "We hope you enjoy your stay with us, Sir. Dinner will be served in the Dining Room at seven. If you should require anything, please use the speaker phone in your room to call down and whoever is on the front desk will deal with your request. Take the gentleman's cases to Room 42, please, Donald." Joe simply nodded, not daring to speak in case his tongue tripped him up.

Their room was located on the first floor just off the balcony they'd seen from below. They could hardly believe the size of it. Ginny's whole cottage would have fit inside and still room to spare! The bellboy placed the cases beside the luggage stand, then held out the keys to Joe who quickly dug some coins out of his pocket and pressed them into the boy's hand and thanked him for his service.

To one side of the room was a vast bed with ornately carved mahogany head and footboards, covered with a gold-coloured, luxurious quilt. Opposite this, was placed a chaise-longue, upholstered in gold velvet to match the bed-linen, beside which stood a small dining table and two chairs. The front of the room consisted almost entirely of several high windows, affording an excellent view over the seafront and the North Sea, with a mirrored dressing table to one side where it would have advantage of the light. Against the rear wall there was a mahogany wardrobe, large enough to take several changes of clothes. This wall also held the door to their own private bathroom complete with a water closet and roll-top bath.

Eva began to unpack their cases, carefully hanging clothes within the wardrobe and placing more intimate garments into the dressing table drawers, while Joe sat on the edge of the giant bed and tried to catch his breath. At last, noticing his silence, Eva returned to his side and pulled herself up to sit beside him. "Penny for them."

"I don't know what to say. I don't belong here, Eva! Did you see all those posh people down there? I'll just end up making a show of myself." Although he didn't say it, he dreaded making Eva ashamed of him. Her father was someone important; she was used to mixing with the well-off; he certainly was not. What had her father been thinking of? He would have been quite content with a smaller hotel or even a boarding house.

Eva turned him towards her, putting her hands either side of his face. She knew better than to tell him he was being silly. "Joe, don't you know I won't see any of those other people. It's the happiest day of my life and I'll only have eyes for you," and she leaned in and kissed him.

Feeling his passion rising, Joe pulled away. Although Eva looked a little hurt by his reaction, he so wanted to do everything properly. It would soon be time to change for dinner, and he intended to spend much more than a few rushed minutes with his new wife.

"Don't you think we should get ready for dinner?"

Eva hid her disappointment behind a bright smile as she collected everything she needed. Joe lay back on the bed and watched her move gracefully about the room. Although not a virgin, he was not so experienced a lover as to feel totally confident about how that evening would go, but he knew enough not to rush things. It was, however, becoming increasingly difficult to control his feelings as Eva took off her going-away outfit so that she stood before him wearing nothing but a silk petticoat before disappearing into the bathroom to complete her toilet.

Eva, on Joe's arm, felt like a princess as they slowly descended the elegant staircase to the hall below. They joined the other guests making their way to the Dining Room, where they were delighted to find they had been allocated a table by the windows with a fine view over the terrace below to the distant harbour. The menu consisted of consommé, followed by oysters, a main course of beef olives with accompanying vegetables, and finishing with Floating Islands dessert. Joe managed to order a decent bottle of cabernet sauvignon with the help of the friendly wine waiter, taking care not to drink too much himself. Not that either of them could have told you much about what they had eaten; both had their thoughts firmly set on the night to come.

Dinner being over by eight thirty, it was still too early to decently retire for the evening, so they decided to return upstairs to the Coffee Room which seemed a little more relaxed than the Grand Ballroom downstairs. This lounge was furnished with numerous tables and comfortable chairs, set about in conversational groups around a more intimate dancefloor, interspersed with potted palms and other ornaments. A string quartet played on a small stage, providing the evening's entertainment.

The aspect of this room was to the South, its tall windows affording fine views over the Spa, but, even though it was still light outside, the drapes had been drawn and the lamps lit, casting a warm glow over guests seated there. Joe and Eva began to relax and talked over the day's events until they judged it safe to disappear back to their room without causing comment. Hand-in-hand they almost raced along the landing in their eagerness, laughing and giggling like two school children on a forbidden mission.

While they had been at dinner, a maid had been in and turned down their bed. Joe took Eva into his arms and kissed her, "Don't be too long, Mrs Fishburn, it's bad form to keep your husband waiting, don't you know?"

Eva laughed at the affected voice he had adopted and replied in kind. "Well, Mr. Fishburn, I'll always do my very best to oblige my husband in all things." Gathering what she needed, she disappeared into the bathroom.

Joe began undressing, hanging his suit in the wardrobe, and self-consciously donning the pyjamas Ginny had insisted he bought. He smiled as he remembered his sister dancing around the room with Jimmy Bell; she'd looked almost young again. Climbing onto the bed, he propped himself on the pillows to await his bride. What could she be doing in there?

Ten minutes later, Eva emerged from the bathroom, draped in a pale pink nightgown which fell in silken folds to the ground. Joe rose to meet her, taking her hands and drawing her into the moonlight spilling from the windows. She was as graceful as one of the alabaster statues that flanked the staircase.

His arms were strong about her, his mouth so sure as he claimed hers for his own. She trembled. How could someone want something so badly yet still be afraid. She did not know what to do; she would do something wrong; she would not be what he wanted.

Joe, whispered into her ear, sensing her fear. "Don't worry my love, I will never do anything to hurt you."

He caught her up and carried her to the bed as if she were no heavier than thistledown; he could almost hear her heart pounding as hard as his own. He lay beside her, stroking her cheek, gazing into her eyes, darkened now with desire. Fighting the fire that kindled deep within him, he forced it down; all he wanted was to please this wonderful creature who was now his soulmate for life.

"I'd like to see you, all of you," he murmured and she acquiesced as he drew the flimsy gown up, over her head before casting it aside. She reached up, slowly undoing his buttons one by one until she could pull his pyjama jacket from him, admiring the rippling muscles of his torso; timidly she loosened his bottoms, pulling them slowly down his thighs, catching her breath as she glimpsed his erect member for the first time. He stifled the urge to shove her back onto the bed, to lay claim to her, to plunder; instead choosing to bring her gently to him as he knelt before her, until their naked bodies touched.

"You are so beautiful, Eva. So soft," and he continued to stroke her, pressed a kiss to her shoulder while his hands gently moulded, caressed, aroused. He was afraid his hands were too big, too rough but his touch was so light, so tender, as his fingers played over her, until she moaned beneath them.

Eva felt as though she were riding on an ocean of feeling; he worked his way over every inch of her heated skin allowing her passion to build until she feared she could endure it no longer. She spoke his name and watched the smile that crossed his lips as he realised she was his alone.

Laying her gently down on the golden quilt, he let his tongue follow where his fingers had lead: over her neck, groaning in pleasure as he suckled each breast while his hand explored her very centre. She grabbed his shoulders and tried to pull him to her, "Now Joe, now!" But he covered her mouth with his, savouring her moans as her passion threatened to overtake them both. Her nails dug into his back as he eased into her, felt her virginity give way to him. He began rhythmically rocking, carrying them to dizzying heights until he felt her body contract, explode into a million stars; she cried out his name as he followed her over the precipice into oblivion.

CHAPTER TWENTY-THREE

When she woke, it took Eva several moments to remember where she was. She reached out her hand to search for her husband, but the bed was empty. Snapping her eyes open, relief flooded through her as she saw him perched on the edge of the bed, already dressed, surveying her silently. "Good morning," she murmured, a smile illuminating her face.

"Good morning, Mrs. Fishburn. I trust you slept well."

Eva giggled; they had had little sleep. "What time is it? Must we get up?"

"It's almost ten o'clock, and yes, we do have to get up. I'm starving, for one thing, and we'll need to get moving if you want to go sightseeing today. Although, seeing you lying there, I could almost be persuaded to spend all day in bed." He moved towards her but she retreated until she could slide off the bed, dragging the quilt with her to cover her naked body.

"Oh no you don't," she squealed. "My mother warned me about men like you who are only after one thing." He lunged for her but she eluded him, swiftly grabbing her nightdress from the floor where it had been discarded the night before and making a beeline for the bathroom.

Joe smiled at her modesty. Where was the little vixen he had slept with last night? He took the speaker phone from its cradle and buzzed reception to ask for breakfast to be brought to their room. He had been awake for over an hour, watching over his wife as she slept peacefully, and he really was ravenous.

By the time breakfast arrived and was laid out on the small table, Eva emerged from the bathroom dressed in a pale blue cotton dress befitting the glorious summer weather. Her eyes shone with happiness and her smile was bright enough to light a room. Delighted with the range of dishes she found underneath silver covers, she was soon tucking into a plate of scrambled eggs with salmon, all the time talking ninety to the dozen about what they might do that day.

Joe, meanwhile, helped himself to a goodly portion of bacon and devilled kidneys before demolishing what was left of the eggs, making sure to nod in all the right places as his wife prattled on. They finished off with toast, smothered in butter and strawberry jam, all washed down with generous cups of tea.

Leaving the front of the hotel, Eva and Joe turned left and joined the other promenaders, crossing the iron bridge and strolling along the Esplanade towards The Spa, a magnificent domed building, made popular by fashionable Victorian society 'taking the waters'. The stylish gardens were filled with couples of all ages enjoying the Sunday morning sunshine. Finding seats before the open bandstand, Joe and Eva settled down to eat their ice creams and listen to the small orchestra as it played a variety of tunes old and new.

Later, they made their way along the sea front to Peasholme Park, wondered at the majestic Japanese pagoda at the top of the hillside walk before finding a good viewing spot to watch the new aquatic display on the lake. Gasps and screams rang out as the guns of the battleships from the Great War resounded, once more defeating the German U-boat. Each vessel was cleverly controlled by a man lying within it. Sitting up on the terraced viewing area, they cheered with the rest of the crowd as the stricken submarine sank to the bottom of the lakebed.

The beaches were crowded with holiday makers and day trippers, seated on deck chairs or towels spread on the golden sand. Many braved the cold of the sea to swim or simply to play around in the waves breaking on the shore. Daring young women barely clothed in the briefest of swimming costumes, sported with young men whose trunks finished well above the knee. Children were everywhere, building castles and sand pies with their buckets and spades, digging their way to Australia, or shrieking with laughter as they rode the donkeys. Joe and Eva strolled along hand-in-hand happy to feel a part of the gaiety around them.

They stopped to lean against the balustrade to watch a group of young men playing football on the beach. "They're just as enthusiastic as the boys at school," Eva said to Joe, experiencing a brief moment of regret that her teaching days were now over. She determined there and then that they would have lots of beautiful children of their own one day.

Suddenly a brightly coloured ball came flying towards them. Eva gave a little scream as she jumped back to avoid it, but she needn't have worried Joe caught it easily. One of the young men was sprinting across the sand towards them. "I say, I'm frightfully sorry. I'm afraid Timmy doesn't know his own strength."

"No harm done," Joe replied before throwing the ball back. With a wave of thanks, the man turned and ran back to his friends. He felt Eva tug at his sleeve. "What's the matter pet?"

"That poor man, did you see his face, Joe? It must

be awful to be so badly scarred like that."

"Probably got it in the war, love. Mebbe his plane caught fire or summat. He certainly sounded posh enough to be a fighter pilot. Anyway, he doesn't seem to let it stop him enjoying life, does he?" He smiled as he watched the group celebrating as one of them scored a goal between the beach towel goalposts.

"I guess you're right. Certainly, beats the alternative, I suppose. So many didn't come back." She shivered at the thought and glanced down at her engagement ring. She was sure Ginny would have loved her Edwin no matter how crippled or disfigured he had been. War was a cruel thing.

Sensing his wife's mood, Joe put his arm around her and turned her away from the seafront. "C'mon, pet, let's away back. My belly's telling me it's getting near dinnertime."

At last they came to the funicular railway and joined the queue to board. It was fascinating watching the smart claret and cream cars working their way up and down the steep cliff, ferrying people between Foreshore Road, which ran the length of the seafront, and Marine Parade on the higher level.

An elderly lady in front of them in the queue turned

around and enquired, "Are you here for a holiday?" Judging by their appearance, she thought they were quite possibly newlyweds. She did so love a wedding.

"Just a short break," Eva smiled back. "We're staying at The Grand."

"I thought I recognised you, you were two tables away from us in the restaurant last night. Perhaps you could join my husband and I for dinner tonight?"

Eva was struggling to find a polite way out of this invitation as Joe evidently was not in agreement by the way he was squeezing her hand. "Well, we'll see. It may be difficult to find a bigger table. The hotel seems quite full."

Luckily, the next car had emptied, and everyone surged forwards. Taking their bench seats, they were amazed at how smoothly the car ascended, affording them magnificent views over the bay.

 Alighting at the top it was only a short walk back to The Grand.

By the time they made their bedroom, it was almost time to get ready for dinner. Eva was determined to make full use of the huge roll top bath; after all, who knew when she would have the chance to bathe in a proper bathroom again? Joe had already kicked off his shoes and was stretched out on the newly-made bed. Obviously, the maid had been in to tidy away the breakfast dishes and make up the bed while they had been out for the day.

"I'm just going to have a quick bath before dinner," Eva said. "I promise not to be too long." Entering the bathroom, she turned the taps on, adding a generous measure of bubble bath from one of the ornate glass bottles, before placing the luxurious bath towel within easy reach. She slipped out of her dress and undergarments and slid thankfully into the steaming water. Lying back, she closed her eyes and dreamt of the night to come. If this was what married life was going to be like, then she would be a very happy wife.

Suddenly, there was a great splash as Joe, divested of his clothing, jumped into the bath with her. Eva shrieked as she felt his feet pushing against her as he struggled to make room for his long legs.

"You didn't think you would get this fine bath all to yourself now, did you?" Joe laughed. "Turn around and I'll wash your back." But before she could do so, he pulled her forwards so that she was sitting astride him, his manhood already swelling, seeking out her perfect centre. Brazenly, she took the initiative; grasping the sides of the bath, she rode him until he lost control, his body rising to meet hers, waves of passion engulfing them as he cried out her name.

They never did make it to dinner. Taking and giving pleasure until the water turned cold, they were forced to retreat to the warm comfort of the double bed, until for a brief time they slept, wrapped in each other's arms.

Hunger drove Joe awake. Reaching over he shook Eva gently and almost succumbed when she moaned softly as she moved into his arms. "C'mon, sweetheart, there'll be enough time for that later. Your husband needs to be fed or he'll run out of stamina!"

Hurriedly dressing, they descended to the seafront via the St. Nicholas Cliff lift conveniently situated to the right of the hotel. Walking quite briskly this time, they soon arrived at the long parade of shops, hotels and entertainments that lined Foreshore Road.

Following their noses, they came to one shop declaring themselves to be selling 'the finest fish and chips' and quickly entered. Joe was dismayed to find the glass warming compartments in front of them were almost empty. Behind the long counter, an elderly gentleman wearing a long white coat, was busily turning fish as it cooked in a deep fryer.

To his left, a younger woman, his daughter perhaps, wore a similar white pinafore, and had her hair protected by a white scarf tied up in a turban.

"What can I get you, Sir?" resting her knuckles on her hips. "I'm afraid there's not much left as we're just about to close. But Dad's just put our own suppers in the pan and you're more than welcome to those."

Eva licked her lips in anticipation. "That's very kind of you. Fish and chips twice, please; just leave them open."

The woman deftly scooped chips into a bag resting on folded newspaper, then slid a piping-hot, golden fish on top, before handing one portion to Eva and another to Joe. "Help yourself to salt and vinegar," she said, indicating the pots standing at one end of the counter. "That'll be two bob, please."

They walked back and sat on the seats in the shelter behind the wrought-iron balustrades. Their silence being testament to the deliciousness of the fare. Scrumpling his empty wrappings into a tight ball, Joe declared, "That was 'grand' as they say hereabouts. That fine food they serve at the hotel is all well and good, Eva, but you can't beat good old fish and chips when you're starving." Eva had to agree with him; whether it was doing without dinner, or the marital activities, that had increased her appetite, she couldn't say, but she had rarely enjoyed a tastier meal in her life.

Although not quite dark yet, Scarborough was beginning to close down for the night. A few determined stragglers still combed the strand; holiday makers made their back to their hotels; one by one the lights were going off in the various establishments along the sea front. Eva and Joe sat arm in arm in companionable silence, watching the moonlight play over the darkening sea.

"Happy?" Joe asked.

"Oh Joe, you've made me the happiest girl in the world. It's a shame we have to go back to the real world tomorrow but, there again, I suppose that's when I really start being Mrs. Joseph Fishburn."

He squeezed her hand tightly and wondered how she was going to cope with the considerable changes there must be in her young, and cosseted, life. "For better or worse?"

Gazing lovingly into his eyes, Eva repeated the words, "For better or worse, Joe, just promise me you'll always love me." She turned her lips up to him to seal their bargain with a tender kiss. "C'mon, husband, it'll soon be time to get up and I've no intentions of you missing breakfast; I'd never hear the last of it!"

CHAPTER TWENTY-FOUR

Roland, taking any opportunity to escape from the shop, met them at Durham Station. they were full of the sights they had seen and described the luxuries of The Grand Hotel in detail. He dropped them off at Ginny's cottage, where they stayed long enough to have a bite of lunch and to collect the rest of Joe's things, before making their way over to Eva's house.

One look at her daughter's face told Bella all she needed to know; Eva fairly radiated happiness, and Joe certainly looked pleased with himself too. While Eva ran upstairs to repack, Joe told Bella all about riding the funicular railway and watching the Naval battle in Peasholme Park. She would have liked to get her daughter alone for a few minutes, but that discussion would have to wait. The young couple were eager to get back to Essingham to get settled into their room at Jean Evans'. Hopefully they shouldn't have too long to wait to be allocated a colliery house of their own.

Thomas was busy slicing a quarter of cooked ham for one of his customers, when they entered the shop. He registered the ting of the bell but didn't look up from his task; a slicer was not a machine with which to take chances. Raising his head, a smile broke over his face and, handing his customer over to Roland to deal with, he hurried around the end of the counter to greet them.

"You're back," he said taking Eva's hands. "Did you have a good time?" He regarded Joe rather sheepishly; he was half expecting to be reprimanded by his new son-in-law for his extravagance but Joe and Eva had already decided to overlook it, just this once. After all they had had a marvellous time.

"It was wonderful, thank you Dad." Eva said, kissing his cheek. "But now it's time to get back to the real world. Roland said it would be alright with you if he gives us a lift back to Essingham."

"Oh but …" Thomas began, but then thought better of it, "Of course he can. I'm sure I can manage without him for another hour, or two," giving his son a meaningful look. "Here, just let me put one or two things in a bag to give Jean and Ellen. It's hard enough making ends meet these days without you two putting onto them." He was filling a bag with eggs and cheese and who knew what else.

"That's very kind of you, err?" Joe was at a loss as to how he should address his father-in-law. He couldn't really call him Mr. Greenall after all.

"Don't you think it's about time you called me Tom?" and to reinforce the relationship he shook

Joe firmly by the hand. "Now, if Roland's finished serving Mrs. Gray, I suggest the pair of you get yourselves away. Your Mam and I will be over to see you on Sunday, and I daresay we'll be bringing Ginny with us. You can tell us all about it then."

"Not all," Eva thought to herself and she squeezed Joe's hand.

In Essingham, Jean Evans' net curtains twitched constantly, as she checked to see if the newly-weds had arrived. They were not surprised, therefore, when they found themselves at the centre of a welcoming committee within ten seconds of pulling up outside Jack and Ellen's house in Bourne Street. Alice threw herself at Joe, who hoisted her up onto his shoulders.

"Fetch your cases in here," Jean said, "then you can get settled for a cup of tea. We're all dying to hear about Scarborough." The men did as they were told, while the women made for the living room, already babbling ninety to the dozen. Alice, unhorsed by Joe, was holding tightly to Eva's hand, determined not to be left out of the gathering.

The kettle was singing on the fire, cups and saucers readied on the table. Ellen passed the baby over to Eva while she went into the back kitchen to slice the

Madeira cake Thomas had sent. Soon everyone was sitting around the room: Joe and Eva relating their adventures; Jack wanting to know how the funicular works; Jean asking about the food served in the hotel; Ellen listening fervently as Eva described the grandeur of the hotel and the fashionable set who graced its halls. Alice sat quietly on Joe's knee, contentedly sucking on a stick of Scarborough rock.

Over the next few weeks the couple settled into their new life. Joe returned to work; Eva spent most of the day helping Ellen with the new baby. Jean was keen to share her wisdom with this young woman who had no experience of running a home or the extra demands a life in mining brought with it.

Underground miners worked four shifts: First, starting at two in the morning, Back from eight 'til three, Nights from three in the afternoon and Ten o'clock night shift. Whatever the shift, a good wife had a hot bath ready in front of the fire and a hearty meal on the table when her husband came home. In houses where there was more than one man working, many women never made it to bed but dozed in a chair between shifts. If she was about, Jean discreetly retreated upstairs while Joe took his bath; she smiled as she listened to the laughter that inevitably accompanied this intimate ritual.

Jean explained to Eva that a woman's standing in the community would be measured by how clean her front step was or how white her nets. The women had little social life beyond the house; it was a brave woman who would venture into a public house. Instead the women would visit each other, sometimes for a cup of tea or, if there was someone left to mind the bairns, they would gather around a frame to prog a clippy mat. On such occasions they might treat themselves to a bottle of sherry, available on draught from the chemist, or a jug of beer from the 'offy': the off licence at one of the local pubs.

Some groups of women organised themselves into 'Knit and Nats' or 'Mothers Clubs' and would meet regularly every week. This was their chance to relax, to have a bit of fun and a laugh amongst friends; to share any worries or swap remedies for common ailments such as chilblains or arthritis. Many also used these clubs as an opportunity to put a bit by out of their weekly housekeeping against a rainy day or to save for something special such as Christmas.

Despite miners having one of the most dangerous jobs, they were not well paid for their labours. If any of the men fell ill or had an accident that kept them from working, they had little to fall back on. No work meant no pay. Despite this the wives always seemed to find some way to put food on the table; quite often relying on the generosity of family and friends in hard times. Eva was welcomed into the hearts of these women, who were only too eager to share their expertise in household management.

One of the things she found difficult were the strange shifts Joe worked. There could be little routine when one week he could be at work all day and the next be gone all night. Whatever his working hours, the days in August were still warm so that they would often take themselves off for long expeditions into the countryside which was barely a stone's throw from the dirty pit.

They explored the densely wooded denes, penetrating deep into the steep sided gorges that ran miles inland. But one of their favourite walks was along the beach banks, the wind fresh on their faces; descending the cliffs to the beaches below; sometimes revisiting the fisherman's hut where they had made tea on Eva's first visit to Essingham; only now taking full advantage of the privacy it afforded. On Sundays, they borrowed Jack's bike and cycled over to Wain Hill to spend a few short hours with Ginny or Bella and Tom before cycling home once again. Bella was especially proud of the way her daughter seemed to be coping with her new life.

One Friday afternoon, at the end of August, Joe burst in waving a piece of paper triumphantly before her face. "We've got a house!" he yelled, almost beside himself with excitement. He swooped Eva up and swung her around and around until she was dizzy.

Laughing, she disentangled herself, forcing him to relinquish his hold on her until she could stand safely on the ground. "Where is it, Joe? Is it close by? When can we see it?"

Jean hurried in from the back kitchen, wiping her hands dry on her pinny. "What's all the todo about in here?"

Joe picked her up too and swung her around once before explaining, "We've been given a house, Jean. I've got the keys right here so's we can gan round and have a look at it this weekend." He took a small bunch of keys from his pocket and held them up for all to see.

Eva reached out and took them from him, reading the cardboard tag attached to them: 18 Court Street. She looked at him fearfully. "There must be some mistake, Joe. This is for a house down East; they're all three bedrooms down there and we don't need three bedrooms, we haven't got a family."

"Aye, that's what I said, but the housing officer said

it was the first one that had come empty since we'd been at the top of the list, so it was ours if we wanted it. 'If we want it?' I says to him, 'course we'll want it.' Then he says, 'well, maybe yee'll need to see if your wife is as keen first.' We have to give him an answer on Monday. Shall we go and see it now, love?"

Jean jumped in, "You will not, Joseph! You'll get your muck off in this bath first, then you'll have the grand dinner your wife has slaved over for you. And you might want to give your Ellen and Jack the good news, before you take yourself off down East. That house will still be there, it's not going anywhere."

As soon as they entered the back yard, Ellen could see the disappointment on Eva's face. There was rubbish piled against the far wall; coal dust lay thick where the coal house had been completely emptied of its contents; water ran incessantly from the toilet overflow drenching everything in its path. The little band picked their way gingerly through the detritus, no-one daring to speak.

Fitting the key into the lock, Joe turned suddenly and scooped Eva up, before opening the door and carrying her over the threshold. Before she had a chance to look around the room, he planted a kiss firmly on her lips then whispered "Welcome home, Love," into her ear. Eva struggled to fight back the tears as she hugged him tightly. There was nothing she could say; what had started out an adventure had turned into a catastrophe.

As usual, it was the plain-speaking Jean Evans who brought everything back into perspective. "We'll soon get this place ship-shape, won't we Ellen? Nowt that a stiff broom and some hot soapy water won't sort out. Look Eva you've one of the new enamelled ranges; no black-leading fireplaces for you, my girl. And at least those young louts haven't put your windows out."

Struggling to free herself from Joe's grasp, Eva crossed to Jean and gave her a huge hug. The house may not be much to look at now but with Ellen and Jean's help, they would soon have it gleaming like a new pin. To cover her embarrassment, Jean barked at the boys, "You two lads go and fetch a barrowload of coal down so's we can get started! Best fetch them two Tilley lamps out of the back of my coalhouse an'all; I don't suppose we'll be able to get the electric back on 'til Monday."

Joe and Jack grinned, only too willing to let someone else take charge for the moment. Without further ado, like a General leading her troops, the little woman, Eva and Ellen toured the rest of the rooms to take stock of what they would need. By the time they were done, the boys were back, the fire was lit and the kettle was on.

Lying in bed that night, Joe reached for Eva. "Happy?"

"I wouldn't quite go that far yet, Joe. But I'm sure we soon will be!"

CHAPTER TWENTY-FIVE

For Eva, 1925 marked the beginning of a new way of life. She and Joe saved every penny they could to make their new house into a comfortable home. Although they found it hard to accept help, many of their family and friends were only too willing to give where they could. Gifts, not in the form of money, but of things people thought might be useful and that they no longer needed, were precious not in a material sense but in the sentiment that lay behind them.

Tom, of course, would have given them all they needed but Bella and Ginny warned him against spoiling the young couple. So, he had to content himself with making sure their larder was never empty. Joe worked as much overtime as was made available to him, but as the year went on this seemed to dwindle.

Eva's days were filled with the continual battle to keep the dirt from the nearby pit at bay. The front step needed to be donkey-stoned until it gleamed; nets had to be regularly dolly-blued to keep them white; backyards and the front street were swilled with the hot water from emptying the wash tub.

Not yet having a tub of her own, Eva carried her

weekly wash up to Ellen's. She packed their few things into a case which could be carried more easily than a bag or sack. Ellen was pleased for the extra help, and, as Jean often popped in from next door, the day passed amicably enough, helped along with numerous cups of tea.

Every Monday, Ellen would be up early to make sure the water was heated in readiness for the weekly ritual. The wash tub was hauled out and filled with steaming water before shavings of carbolic soap were added. Whites first, then coloureds, then darks and finally pit clothes. By the time this routine was completed the water often resembled the black slurry that issued in a continuous stream from the pit workings onto the beach below. The filthy water was run off into a bucket and, if it was deemed too dirty to swill the paths, was poured down the sink in the back yard.

Then the whole process began again as the clothes were rinsed in clean water. Ellen was lucky enough to have a mangle to squeeze out most of the water from their garments; many weren't and had to manage best they could by wringing the clothes out by hand. Eva stretched the washing line across the front street between the rows of houses and then hung the washing out to dry. To see streets filled with lines of blowing sheets reminded Eva of a painting she had once seen of a fleet of ships sailing into battle.

Women prayed for fine windy weather on washdays as the alternative meant drying everything on clothes horses in front of the fire or on pulleymaids slung from the ceiling. As a result the rooms would be humid all day, with water often running down the windows and sometimes even the walls.

Other women preferred to use the communal laundry which was situated at the top of the green behind Seaside Lane. Here, for a shilling, you could use the sinks and tubs provided, but you had to take your own pail of coal to heat the water and then carry the heavy bags of wet washing back home to dry; it was an arduous task. Still, as with most things, the women made the best of it. In their bright wrap-around pinnies, hair protected by headsquare turbans, chattering away, Eva thought they resembled a cage full of budgerigars.

Dinner on washdays was usually Tatie 'ash; this consisted of the left-over meat from the Sunday roast chopped up and added to a large pan of potatoes, onions, carrots and turnip, immersed in water with a couple of Oxo cubes added to make the gravy. This could then be set aside until an hour or so before the men were due in from work and put to boil ready for dinner.

In Summer, washing done and hung out to dry, dinner prepared, Ellen and Eva took the opportunity to pull out chairs to sit outside the front door, basking in the sun and passing a few minutes gossiping with neighbours. A woman's lot may be a hard one in these colliery communities, but Eva found the women took every opportunity to socialise and by September she knew many of other wives, at least to nod to in passing.

For Joe it was a relief that his wife seemed to be settling in quite well to her new life. When he was around during the day, they went for long walks or worked together up on the allotment. Although by no means luxurious, they had everything they needed to make their life comfortable enough and a growing circle of friends so that Eva rarely remembered to feel homesick.

As the nights drew in, the worsening weather drove them indoors, either listening to the radio or spending evenings playing cards at Jack and Ellen's or the home of one of their other friend's. Christmas was fast approaching and Eva worked hard making decorations for the house and Christmas cards to send to family and friends. Jean sat patiently with her, teaching her how to knit and she was becoming a master with a proggy hook, evidenced by the colourful rug that now sat in front of her coal range.

One night when several couples were gathered in Jack and Ellen's, Ellen announced rather shyly that she was once again pregnant. One look at Jack's face told everyone how proud he was.

"I dunno, Jack, seems you just have to hang your pants on the bottom of the bed and your poor wife is havin' another babby," Tom Higgins joked, although he hardly had room to talk: he and Ada had been married seven years and Ada was carrying their fourth child.

"Aye well," Jack countered, "if you ask me it's about time young Joe here was showing us what he's made of."

Joe snorted his derision but refused to countenance the comment with a response. Eva hung her head, trying to hide her obvious embarrassment as she blushed scarlet.

"Leave our Joe alone, you two," Ellen said, ever quick to champion her younger brother. "Pay them no mind Eva. If you ask me, I wouldn't be in too much of a rush to tie meself down with squawking kids, there's plenty of time for that when you're an old maid like me."

"Don't worry Ellen, we want a bit more behind us

before we'd even consider starting a family; isn't that right Pet?"

Eva said nothing but simply nodded her agreement. Maybe Joe would have to change his opinion soon, she thought.

Later that night as they lay in each other's arms, Eva returned to the subject. "You know when you said we didn't want to start a family yet, Joe, how long were you thinking we should wait?"

Raising himself on one elbow he regarded his wife quizzically. "Well I don't really know; we haven't really discussed it much, have we? What do you think?"

"Erm," she hesitated, "Would it be so bad if we had a baby sooner rather than later?"

"Do you think you could manage looking after a baby as well as the house? I know you've had to cope with a lot of change since we got married. But if you've got your mind set then we'll have to see what we can do." He leaned over so that he could nuzzle that soft spot behind her ear that she so liked but she pushed him back.

"I think you've already done more than enough, Joseph Fishburn!" she said trying her best to adopt her stern teacher's voice but failing miserably, a giggle escaping unbidden from her lips.

Joe looked puzzled; it took a moment or two for the penny to drop. "Do you mean…?"

Eva nodded. "I'm almost certain, but I won't know for sure until I see the doctor." If she had been worried that he might be angry or upset by her news, any such thoughts were soon dispelled by the look of sheer joy on his face.

He pulled her into his arms and held her so tightly she could hardly breathe. "You clever, clever girl."

"We can't tell anyone 'til we're certain, Joe. I'll make an appointment to see the doctor but even then I'd like to wait a while to make sure everything is going to be alright before we make it general knowledge."

"But we will be able to tell your Mam and Dad and our Ginny and Ellen, won't we?" He was so proud, he didn't know if he would be able to keep their secret for long.

"Of course, anyway I daresay Ellen will soon twig when I start feeling tired or worse being sick every morning. So, I take it you don't mind not waiting to start a family, then?"

"Let me show you just how much I mind," and his mouth sought hers eagerly. Starting a family, bringing a helpless baby into this world who would be totally dependent on them was more than a little frightening, but Joe knew that never had he loved his wife more than at this moment.

CHAPTER TWENTY-SIX

Joe and Stan were sitting with their backs firmly set against a prop at the kist. Joe had been rather quiet, which prompted Stan to ask, "Everything alreet at home, marra?"

"Aye, everything's fine, how's that like?"

"Well, there's hardly been a word out of you all shift; a thowt mebbe thy lass was feelin' a bit poorly."

"No, Eva's in fine fettle now she's stopped being sick in the mornings. Pregnancy seems to suit her; she's getting' a right little tummy on her now."

Stan didn't like to pry but his friend obviously had something on his mind and Stan knew the dangerous nature of their work needed everyone's full attention. "Well there's summat yer bothered about, out with it."

"Have you heard all the talk about a walk out, Stan? Ah can't afford to loss work, not with a babby on the way."

"Aye, it certainly looks like we'll be coming out. No-one trusts Baldwin to see us right once the subsidy ends. They should never have handed the pits back to the owners after the war; they are just lookin' for the chance to cut our wages and make us work longer hours. Nationalisation was the only chance we had to get a fair day's pay and the pits to be modernised."

"But things aren't so bad here in these newer pits agin the coast, Stan, although I must say conditions were pretty bad down Brampton where I worked afore I came here."

"The majority of pits are still using pick and shovel to get the coal out, Joe. Our leaders in the Federation are set to fight for a better future. Let's just hope the steelworkers and the railwaymen stand with us this time or we might be fighting a losin' battle again on us own. We'd best get back to work before Bert puts in an appearance; if we get the sack neither of us will have to worry about comin' out on strike."

With a heavy heart, Joe hung his coat back up on the prop behind him. All he could do was hope that their Union leaders and the government could find some agreement with the coal owners. It wasn't the best time to be bringing a new life into a world filled with such uncertainty.

Meanwhile, back in Bourne Street, Eva and Ellen were taking a welcome break from the weekly wash. "Have you decided where you're going to have your baby yet, Eva?" Ellen asked, pouring tea into the two cups set upon the table.

"My Mam and Dad want me to go into the Cottage Hospital, but I'd much rather stay at home. You've had both yours at home and had no trouble so I don't see what all the fuss is about."

"They're only worried for you, Eva; it's understandable, it's their first grandchild after all. And it must be hard for your Mam being so far away."

"You'll never guess what Mam's done, Ellen; she's got Dad giving her driving lessons so she can come over more often. I wouldn't like to be a passenger in the car with them when Dad starts trying to tell her what to do," chuckling, she took a biscuit from the plate and dunked it in her tea.

"What does Joe think?" Ellen prompted.

"Oh him! He is trying to keep out of it, as usual. I think he wouldn't mind if I went to hospital to have it but we can't afford it and you know what he's like about accepting 'charity' off my Dad. I think I'll sort out with Mrs. Hailes to have it at home. There's not much she doesn't know about delivering babies and she'll stay and do a bit housework and make Joe's meals too. If it does start to look like there'll be any complications, then the Doctor can always book me in with the midwife later. You'll be having yours at home I suppose?"

"Aye. The more you have, the easier it gets they reckon and I've never had any bother in the past."

Just then, there was a sharp knock on the back door and Jean Evans flew in, closing the outside door smartly behind her. "Eee it's freezing out there. Any tea left in that pot, pet, I'm gasping."

"Come in Jean and take your coat off. You'll be hard pressed to get to the fire, though, 'cause I've had to put the washing to dry on the clothes horse; it'd freeze stiff as a board if I tried to hang it out today."

"You sit yourself still, chick, I'll sort meself out." She nipped back into the scullery to get another cup, pulled out a chair from the table and made herself comfortable. The next ten minutes were taken up with the latest gossip gleaned from her morning's expedition to the various shops up Station Road.

Finally, Eva interjected, "We'll have to get on with this washing, Ellen, or my Joe will be in and no dinner on the table. You know what he gets like if he's not fed." She grimaced in imitation of Joe's hungry face.

"You get yourself off, if you like Eva. I'll stay and finish the washing with Ellen and fetch your things down later. It's a while since I've seen Joe. I must say the house seems empty without the pair of you getting under me feet."

"We'll all be seeing far too much of our men if they walk out again," Ellen said grimly.

Jean looked up sharply, "I do hope it doesn't come to that. I remember what it was like in nineteen twenty-one, and in nineteen ten afore that. Everyone going without and for what? There'll be no besting the owners while the Tories are in power. Those toffs all stick together." One look at Eva's stricken face made her wish she had held her tongue; she was sure the lass had never had to go without for even one day in her life. And her with a baby on the way too. "No matter what we'll all pull through and with a bit of luck it'll not come to that.

"Now make sure you wrap up, Eva, it's perishing out and that wind's bitter coming straight off the water."

Eva walked briskly down the street, her hands pushed deep into her coat pockets. As she walked her mind was in turmoil: would the men come out on strike? how would they manage for money with no wage coming in? what would this mean for their baby? She knew her parents would not let them starve but she also knew that any dispute would mean leaner times for her father's business too.

Well, for the moment at least she could still put a hearty meal of mince and dumplings on the table for her husband coming in. Tomorrow would have to take care of itself.

Ginny sat in her chair beside the fire, knitting baby clothes. It was obvious that she was expecting company as the table was set with cups and saucers for afternoon tea; a plate of freshly made scones nestled under a tea towel.

Hearing a car pull up, she rose from her seat and went to open the door. Outside, Bella and Tom were engaged in a healthy discussion about the quality of Bella's driving.

"You must remember to apply your handbrake as soon as the car comes to a stop!" an exasperated Tom was telling his wife.

"Alright, alright but we were on the flat so there was no harm done. I would have put it on if you had given me a chance."

"But if you were on the slightest of inclines, the car would have rolled back. That is how accidents happen."

Bella let out what could only be described as a snort, before turning to her friend. "Ginny will you tell this pompous old fool not to be so pedantic. He'll give himself a coronary if he isn't careful."

Ginny laughed. "Come in the pair of you; it's much too cold for doorstep disputes today." Turning, she lead the way indoors, closing the door firmly behind them. "Are you staying for a cup of tea, Tom? If so get yourself another cup off the dresser."

"Well, just a quick one. There's something we need to discuss."

Intrigued, Ginny took the boiling kettle off the fire and mashed the tea in the large brown teapot. She wondered what bee Tom had in his bonnet now?

Once they were seated round the table armed with cups of tea and delicious buttered scones generously topped with home-made strawberry jam, she waited for him to begin.

"Not to put too fine a point on it. Ginny, what chance do you think we have in persuading our Eva to come home to have this baby?"

Ginny's eyes bulged in disbelief.

"Before you say anything, just let me say that we know she is very happy with Joe and he would never knowingly let any harm befall either Eva or the baby but that's not the same as being here where Dr. Whittington, who has been our family doctor for many years, can deliver the baby or get her to hospital quickly if things go wrong." Thomas seemed to run out of steam at last.

"And what do you think, Bella?"

"Personally, I don't think he's got a cat in hell's chance but you know what he's like when he gets his teeth into something. I've told him your Ellen has had two babies in Essingham and nothing untoward has happened to her or the babies. Eva is a fit and healthy young woman and there should be no reason why anything should go wrong."

"But what if…" Thomas seemed to have found a second wind but Ginny held up a hand to stop him mid-sentence.

"Tom, I think if you so much as try to interfere you'll simply make Eva more determined to go her own way, she is your daughter, after all." Ginny gave him a very knowing look. "Essingham has a perfectly good Cottage Hospital of its own and Eva has every faith in her own doctor. She is a very educated and clever young lady and even if she decides to have the baby at home, then you must accept that it's up to her and Joe."

Thomas opened his mouth to say something else but

thought better of it. Bella looked very pleased with herself as she regarded her floundering husband.

"Now drink your tea and leave me and Bella in peace so we can have a good chinwag."

Knowing he was soundly beaten, odds of two to one being definitely against him, Tom did as he was bidden, promising to return in a couple of hours to pick his wife up.

Ginny cleared the dishes from the table, putting them in the sink to wash up later. "Come and sit by the fire Bella, and tell me how your driving lessons are doing," she smiled at her friend.

"First, I think we should make plans as to what we should do if this blessed strike comes off. We've both been around long enough to know that no-one ever comes out the winner really. I know Tom will see our two alright, although he'll be trying to help out everyone by extending them more credit than we can really afford, but I think it's up to us older ones to organise the women into setting up soup kitchens to help feed the worst off."

Ginny nodded her agreement. "Let's just hope the government see sense and make the owners toe the line as far as paying the miners what they are worth. Heavens knows it's a filthy and dangerous enough job they do without expecting them to do it on starvation wages."

"I can't see it myself. I wouldn't be surprised if the Tories are just buying time, putting off the men for as long as possible so's they can be ready for the next strike. Churchill will certainly give his backing to the owners." Bella's father being a banker, she had seen first-hand what strikes did to destroy not just families but whole communities. She shivered as she thought what the possible consequences might be for her family if the miners were driven once again into action.

CHAPTER TWENTY-SEVEN

Christmas came and went without a great deal of festive spirit. Everyone tried to keep things normal for the children's sakes, but with the thoughts of strike looming, most sought to save as much as they could towards the coming hardship. On New Year's Eve, far from looking forward to a healthy and prosperous year to come, most prayed that they would get through it in one piece.

As New Year's Day fell on a Friday, Joe would not go back to work after the Christmas shutdown until the following Monday, so he and Eva decided to spend New Year's Eve with Thomas and Bella. It was quite a relief to gain a brief respite from the increasingly sombre faces of their friends and neighbours. They were both resigned to the fact that there was little likelihood of any settlement being reached when the subsidy ceased at the end of April, but for one night they could put that aside and enjoy themselves with their family.

Thomas, only too well aware of what a protracted strike could mean to them all, was determined to put on one last show before they all had to draw in their purse-strings. The table was heavily laden with festive food and the drinks cabinet fairly groaned under the weight of bottles of spirits and mixers waiting to make the latest cocktails.

Roland was to be in charge of the music; a stack of records donated by his friends standing ready by his record player. The dining room carpet had been rolled up to leave a decent dance floor in the centre of the room, the furniture having been vacated or pushed back against the walls.

As the guests began to arrive, the air was one of eager anticipation. Everyone looked to have made an extra effort: girls and women dressed in their finery and men, young and old, looking groomed and handsome. If some of the smiles seemed a little forced, then no-one commented on it.

Eva, had resisted her mother's pleas to allow her to buy her a new party dress. Approaching the fifth month of her pregnancy, her clothes were beginning to feel rather tight around her swelling waistline, but in such uncertain times, she could not justify spending good money on fripperies. Instead, Ginny had made a fine job of letting out the seams on a few of her old dresses, enough to see her through in the short-term at least. It wasn't as if she would have much call for dressing-up in the near future, after all.

Joe, looked handsome as ever in his wedding suit. Eva was glad now that her father had not had his way over hiring morning suits for their wedding.

Her parents too, had shown restraint in so far as her mother contented herself with selecting a dress from the many infinitely suitable gowns already hanging in her wardrobe. Even Thomas had tamed his extravagance for once, merely adding a new white collar to his ensemble. With Stan's outfit comprising baggy trousers, shirt and pullover sported by many of the fashionable young set, the family looked the epitome of good taste.

Earlier, while they were upstairs dressing, Bella sat Eva down on the bed, grabbing the opportunity to have a few private words with her daughter. "You know that your father and I are so proud of you, Eva, and so happy for you and Joe; a baby is a very precious thing. But you must promise if you need anything, you will ask, won't you darling? I know how stubbornly independent you can be; just like your father."

"Don't worry, Mum, we'll manage just fine. Ginny is knitting and sewing enough garments to clothe a dozen babies, and I hear even you have mastered a crocheting hook." Eva couldn't help but smile as she pictured her mother studiously bent over the fine white shawl she was making for her first grandchild. "You must try to keep Dad on a tight rein for me, though, or he'll be trying to buy out

Fenwick's if you don't stop him."

"Just you leave your father to me, girl. You know how much he loves to spoil you but I daresay you will have to take a back seat when this new baby arrives."

"I know he means well but Joe has enough to worry about at the moment without Dad making it worse."

"Have you made any arrangements for the birth, yet? Will you be going into hospital?"

"I hope not, Mum. We'd like to have it at home. I've booked Mrs. Hailes to come in and deliver; she's delivered both of Ellen's without any bother; although, if there's the least sign of any complications she'll send straight for Dr. Johnson of course. He's really nice and quite young so he's right up to the minute with the latest medical developments."

"Is Mrs. Hailes the local midwife then?"

"Well, she's what they call a bona fide midwife; she's been delivering babies forever. There's not much you can tell her about childbirth, she's seen it all. The colliery women swear by her; whether it's one coming into the world or one going out, everyone sends for Mrs. Hailes."

Bella looked rather shocked; of course, she knew

there such women in their village but she wasn't sure about her own daughter being dependent on one. Maybe Thomas had had the right idea after all.

By ten o'clock the party was in full swing. The young ones and even one or two of the older generation, were dancing enthusiastically in the dining room while those who preferred a rather calmer atmosphere retired to the more comfortable setting of the living room.

Generous plates of food were eaten, washed down by somewhat copious amounts of alcohol. As the evening wore on everyone began to relax. For one night 1926 would have to take of itself; they were determined to see 1925 out in style. As the final minutes of the old year ticked away, Joe and Roland were dispatched to wait outside to be admitted as first foots. It seemed the whole world stood still, waiting with bated breath for Big Ben to chime midnight on the radio. Who knew what thoughts, past, present and future, were on peoples' minds?

As the final stroke of twelve was struck, everyone let out a great cheer; Joe and Roland were admitted, armed with their pieces of coal to throw on the fire for luck. Each was given a silver coin, a glass of whiskey and piece of spice as a reward for their labours. Then all joined hands in a circle to sing 'Auld Lang Syne'.

Joe took Eva in his arms and kissed her deeply. Looking into her eyes he said, "I love you, Mrs. Fishburn. Let's hope this year turns out to be a good one after all."

Eva replied, "I love you too, Mr. Fishburn. We have so much to be thankful for and no matter what life throws our way we'll see it through together."

As they turned back to the rest of the room, Joe's eyes nearly popped out of his head at the sight of his sister, Ginny, and Jimmy Bell engaged in what could only be termed a passionate embrace, under the mistletoe which was suspended from the light fitting in the centre of the room.

"Well would you look at that!" he said to Eva. "Maybe I will have to have a serious chat with Jimmy and discover just what his intentions are."

Laughing, Eva kept tight hold of his arm to prevent him from marching over to the couple there and then. "I would have thought his intentions are perfectly clear, Joe. But I wouldn't worry too much; if you ask me, Ginny seems to be in total control of the situation." Perhaps, she thought, it was as well that they were sleeping at her parent's house that night. It was about time Ginny had some fun in her life.

CHAPTER TWENTY-EIGHT

January is a depressing month in the coalfields. Joe especially hated working dayshift when he hardly saw the sun all week. "We're more like moles than men," he complained to Eva. Even if he could have got up to the allotment, there was little to do there; few plants could survive the harsh conditions as temperatures plummeted and the ground froze. Joe and Jack took it in turns to trek up the cliff to Paradise Gardens to feed the hens and collect the meagre few eggs they laid. At least it was an excuse to escape the house for a while, meeting up in one of the sheds or pigeon lofts with other miners to discuss the latest developments, or rather lack of them, in the negotiations with the coal owners.

Many men still frequented the local pubs but Joe and Jack were saving as much as they could, both would soon have another mouth to feed. The few improvements Eva and Joe had planned for their new home had had to be put on hold until the dispute was settled. Even the Pitch and Toss square along the black path on the other side of the railway tracks had fewer visitors.

Eva too was feeling depressed. The initial excitement of being pregnant was gradually being eclipsed by worries about the actual birth. This wasn't helped by some of the women who seemed to take delight in regaling her with some of their own personal horror stories. Ellen and her mother had both told her to ignore them but that was easier said than done.

Women's work was hard at any time of the year: trying to keep the dirt of the pit at bay was no easy task. Washing could rarely be hung out on the street lines to dry: it froze solid in the freezing winds blowing straight off the North Sea. Instead everything was dried on a clothes horse in front of the kitchen fire, leaving the house damp for days.

The houses were heated solely by the range. Eva pulled their chairs up as close as possible to the fire and hung thick curtains over the outside doors to keep out draughts. To save coal, none of the other fires in the house were lit; every morning the bedroom windows were frosted with delicate lace patterns. The morning visit to the toilet was by necessity a brief one; their breath steaming as they hurried down the yard.

It seemed the only ones who were immune to the Winter were the children who played out from morning until long after dusk. They built barricades out of the snow that avalanched off the roofs and fought epic snowball battles. Many of the women cursed them as they created slides on the icy-smooth pavements running down the hills between the rows of houses.

Some lucky kids had fathers who managed to trade bundles of chopped sticks or cigarettes for sledge irons forged in the blacksmith's shop. Topped with bits of wood, these sledges could be seen hurtling at breakneck speed down the long bank running from the cemetery, down the full length of North, to the pit itself. The children whose sledges were big enough to carry three or four at a time found themselves to be suddenly very popular.

Returning home briefly for food or to quickly replace wet socks and gloves if available, the children collapsed into bed each night exhausted but happy. Their faces reddened by the cold, they were inevitably dosed by their mothers with thick cough syrup and had their hands and feet rubbed with greasy homemade remedies to ward off chilblains.

As January gave way to February everyone welcomed the warmer weather and the lengthening days. It was Monday and Eva had just returned from doing her washing at Ellen's. Joe would complain when he came home; he thought she shouldn't be carrying the heavy case of wet washing in her condition. She was arranging the clothes on the clothes horse around the fire, when she heard the loud blast of a car horn outside her front door.

Running to the front room window, she drew back the nets and was delighted to see her mother getting out of the car. Quickly opening the front door, she ushered her inside before the cold could rush in. Bella took off her coat and hat and hung them on the hooks at the bottom of the stairs, before following her daughter into the warm kitchen.

"Get the kettle on, there's a good girl. The heater in that car is worse than useless."

Eva was standing open-mouthed. "Did you drive all this way on your own, Mum? Does Dad know?" She could not imagine that her father would have entrusted her mother with his car.

"Of course, I did! You and your father should have a little more faith in my driving skills, Eva." Looking at her daughter's shocked face, she continued, "He'll know I've gone the minute he gets in from work and finds my note propped up on the mantelpiece. I dare say he won't be happy about it mind, but he'll be fine when he realises I've left his dinner plated up for him to reheat in the oven."

"Oh Mum, he'll go crazy with worry. I wouldn't be surprised if he drives straight over here in the shop van."

"He wouldn't dare! He knows perfectly well that I am a safe and competent driver. I just had to take the bull by the horns and prove it to him that's all."

"But it will be dark soon. Have you ever driven at night before, Mum?"

"No, and I don't intend to now. If it's alright with you and Joe, I've brought a few things so I can stay for a day or two. I hardly see you these days. A girl needs her mother at times like these."

Eva had to smile as she thought of her father storming around the house ranting to no-one but himself. No doubt Roland would suffer the brunt of it when he got in. She had to admit, however, that it was comforting to know that her mother could be there quickly if she needed her and it would be nice to spend some time alone with her.

Joe was delighted to have Bella to stay for as long as she wanted. He was aware that as her pregnancy progressed, Eva often felt the need for a woman's company and although she was even closer to her sister-in-law than ever, Ellen was almost full-term now and finding everything more tiring. When he was in ten o'clock shift, it would be reassuring to him if Eva was not left alone all night while he was working.

By the middle of March, everyone felt the benefit as the days lengthened and the weather turned distinctly warmer. Taking advantage of the warm

Spring sunshine, Eva was outside cleaning her front windows when she saw Mrs. Hailes heading down the street towards her.

"Now then young lady," Mrs. Hailes greeted her brightly, "I've just had word to go to your Ellen's; it's her time. I thought you might like to come and give me a hand."

Eva got down heavily from the cracket, wiping her hands on her pinny. "Of course, just let me grab my coat and leave a note for Joe in case I'm not back before he gets in." She was already half-way through the door, stripping her pinny off as she went to get ready. In a couple of minutes she was back and the two women hurried up the bank together.

They found Ellen already in bed, apparently well-on in her labour; indeed, Jean Evans was just replacing the thick layer of newspaper, blanket and top sheet covering a rubber sheet, that was meant to save the mattress from the necessary mess of childbirth. Although Jean had never had a child herself, she had helped Molly Hailes bring many babies into the world and was well versed in what to do.

"Ee I'm pleased to see you Molly; 'er waters have gone; it'll not be long now, I reckon."

Eva crossed to the bed and took hold of her sister-in-law's hand. She had never attended a birth before and was quite concerned at Ellen's appearance. She was lying back on her pillows obviously exhausted: her face red and sweaty; her long hair, usually tied up in a tight bun, fell loose and dishevelled around her shoulders.

"How are you doing, Ellen?" Eva enquired and was relieved to see a smile spread weakly over Ellen's face.

"I'm fine, Eva. Are you sure you want to be here, though? I don't want to put you off; it's not a pretty business, havin' a baby." She thought Eva looked like a scared rabbit sitting there beside her. She felt Eva wince, as she automatically tightened her grip on her friend's hand as she felt the onset of another contraction. The pains were stronger now and she could only hope the end was near.

"It'll do her good to know what's ahead of her. Shame on you Ellen Surtees, there's no better sight than another soul entering this world. Now let's see how things are getting along." Molly Hailes waited until the contraction had passed then positioned herself between Ellen's legs. "The head's crowning nicely, another couple of pains should do it.

Eva glanced down nervously to the foot of the bed. Mrs Hailes might seem brusque and matter-of-fact, but she could tell from the woman's demeanour and

Ellen's response to her ministrations that she was also the gentlest of nurses. She found this very reassuring, after all this was the woman who would be delivering her own precious baby.

A few minutes later, everything seemed to gain momentum. "Now Ellen, when the next pain comes I don't want you to push but take little short breaths so we can bring the head slowly; we don't want to squash the bairn's head any more than we have to."

Eva almost held her breath as she felt Ellen's fingers begin to tighten around her own. "Here it comes," she managed to squeeze out before the next pain hit her.

"Right dearie, now pant! Keep panting!" Eva didn't know exactly what was happening but she could see that Molly was totally absorbed in delivering the baby's head safely. "Good girl!" Molly praised Ellen. "Take a rest pet. When the next pain comes I'm gonna want you to push. You ready?"

Eva watched entranced as Ellen pushed with all her might; her sweet face contorted with pain and exertion as Molly skilfully guided first one shoulder, then the other through the swollen vulva. Then suddenly it was there! A perfect baby boy, rather blue perhaps and covered in a bloody mess but nevertheless quite the most beautiful baby Eva had ever seen.

Molly quickly took a short rubber tube and cleared the baby's airways of any mucous. Then deftly, she cut and tied the cord, wrapped the baby in a clean white towel and placed him in Ellen's waiting arms. It seemed to Eva that everyone bar Molly was crying, their tears stemming from a mixture of relief, joy and wonder at the miracle they had all experienced.

CHAPTER TWENTY-NINE

It was round about this time that Joe locked horns with Ned Sherringham for the first time. The team were working the back shift and were surprised to learn that Bert Soulsby, their regular Deputy, had reported in sick and Ned Sherringham, being an Acting Deputy, would be overseeing production on the face in his place.

As soon as Stan recognised the man waiting for them at the kist, he gave Joe the heads up. "Watch this one, Joe. He's got a chip on his shoulder you could build a house with."

Joe quickly appraised the man; there was nothing remarkable about him: he was of average height and build but he marked the weasly blue eyes now regarding him suspiciously from beneath the deputy's leather cap. "You'll be that new lad, Joe Fishburn." He made it sound more of an accusation than a greeting. Joe nodded in reply. "I dunno why we keep takin' on you Woolybacks. There's plenty of good lads round here wantin' jobs without bringin' in outsiders," he sneered.

"Leave the lad be, Ned," Stan interrupted, "he does his job, you do yours and stop looking for trouble just 'cos ye've been made a deputy for a day."

The colour rose sharply in Ned's cheeks but he knew better than to tangle with Stan Barlow. He held his peace but thought if any of these jumped-up canchmen put a foot out of line on his watch, he'd show them who was boss. Turning on his heel, he stomped off towards the coalface.

"What's his problem then?" Joe asked. He was unused to being treated so harshly by someone he had never even met.

"Ned? He had an older brother, Seth, killed on The Somme. The apple of his father's eye, Seth was. They reckon Ned's tryin' to live up to his memory; to prove to his Ma and Da he's just as big a man as his brother was. Me? I reckon he's just a nasty piece of work. Best you steer clear of him, Joe. As you can see, he doesn't like anyone comin' in from outside the village."

"It'll be hard to keep out of his way if he's gonna be our Deputy, Stan."

"Let's just hope there's nowt much wrong with Bert then, and that he's back to work Monday."

Fred appeared at the entrance to the coal face. "See Ned's in 'is usual 'appy mood," he said, "He's got a face on would curdle the milk. Right, let's get this lot cleared and made safe; nee need to give 'im owt else to twist about."

Joe would have been quite content to leave Ned well alone, but fate often has a strange way of intervening. Later that same week their paths crossed again. The Leathercap Club was established as a place for officials of the colliery to socialise over a friendly pint or two. It was situated at the bottom of Bourne Street so was a very convenient watering hole for the two men. Joe and Jack couldn't be members because they weren't officials of the pit, but they could still drink there if one of the members signed them in, although they themselves weren't allowed to buy alcohol from the bar.

On Friday, Joe and Jack spent an agreeable evening playing dominoes with Bert and another Deputy, Jim Baker. Joe didn't like to go out and leave Eva on her own now she was so far on but Bella was staying over and the two women had almost pushed him out of the door.

At ten o'clock, Joe pushed his chair back and rose to his feet somewhat unsteadily. "Thanks for a good evening, lads. I'd best get home afore my supper's on the fireback." He was pulling on his coat as he made his way out of the front door, when he accidently bumped into someone entering. "Ay sorry mate, didn't see you there." The smile froze on his face as he recognised the other man.

"Why don't you watch where you're goin'?" Ned Sherringham growled. "Any road, what d'ye think yer doin' in here? You're not an official."

Joe could have reminded Ned that he wasn't an official either; he was only acting deputy after all. Instead he simply apologised again for colliding with him. But it seemed Ned wasn't willing to let it go. "Yer all the same you woolybacks," he snarled, "think yer better than anyone else but ye've got nee spine when it comes to it."

By now Ned had his face pushed right up to Joe's, although he had to stand almost on tip-toes to reach the bigger man. Joe decided he had had enough of this bully; if it was a fight he wanted, he was ready to give him one. He was just about to get hold of the other man's lapels, when he felt a firm hand on his shoulder.

"Alright Joe?" Jack paused, relieved when he felt some of the tension leave his brother-in-law's shoulders. "This toe-rag giving you bother?"

Ned's gaze shifted to the three men who now stood behind Joe. He didn't like the odds and quickly decided to back off, retreating to a much safer non-threatening distance, uttering, "Just watch yourself in future!" before pushing past them to enter the bar. It didn't help that the whole bar could hear the laughter that was directed at Ned's back as he scuttled away.

By the time he got home, Joe's temper had cooled, and he was whistling as he opened the back door into the kitchen. Eva and Bella sat either side of the fire listening to the radio. Joe bent to plant a kiss on his wife's waiting lips.

"Urgh, you stink of beer Joe. No need to ask if you've had a good night."

"A've only had a couple, pet. Played a great game of dominoes with the lads, who, I may add, begged me to stay for 'just one more' but I said 'No, my beautiful wife will be waitin' patiently for me.' So I left them and came straight home to you." He tried to snatch another kiss but she was ready for him and pushed him back.

"Get away with you. More likely you were frightened to roll in here in a drunken state and face my Mam."

Joe caught Bella's hands and dragged her onto her feet and proceeded to waltz her around the cramped kitchen. Bella laughed at the pair of them even as she protested, "Stop it, you daft fool. You'll have us both on the floor in a minute."

Depositing Bella back into her seat by the fire, he turned back to Eva. "Is there owt for supper, pet, or is your poor owld husband to go to bed hungry?"

"There's a bit of corned beef pie in the oven, though you don't deserve it."

Bella retrieved the pie from the oven and put it on a plate for Joe, then made him a mug of tea. "Right, I'm off to bed. Don't you two stop up all night. I'll see you in the morning before I set off home." As she climbed the steep staircase she smiled, 'This is what it's all about: family.' Soon there would be a baby to make it complete. Could life be any better?

CHAPTER THIRTY

Spring 1926 seemed to match the mood of the colliery men and women: wet and miserable with little to smile about. Whatever the possible outcome of the dispute, everyday life must continue. Men tunnelled in the earth; women cared for hearth and home; allotments were dug over and planted.

Union meetings were held in Miners' Welfare Halls throughout the country where leaders tried to keep the men abreast of any developments and strengthen their resolve to resist pressure from the coal owners to reduce wages and lengthen working hours.

After such meetings, the men often met up in the Working Men's Club further up the hill. This magnificent building, opened in 1920, reflected the solidity and strength of the miners who drank there. Gathering in the concert room, discussions centred around the coming strike.

"It said in the paper that the TUC still didn't believe the government will let it come to a strike. I must say I can't see how the country's ganna manage without any coal. The factories will all be at a standstill; the trains won't be able to run and everyone needs coal to heat the water and cook the food, don't they?" The elderly speaker took off his cap and scratched at his sparsely covered head as he struggled to make sense of the situation.

"Aye but we all know they've been stockpiling coal for the last eight months since they bought the owners off with the wages subsidy. And people don't need coal so much in the Summer, now, do they? If only the government could see the way clear to insisting the owners modernise the old pits, like what's happenin' owr in Germany, then we could get the coal out as cheap as they do."

"Good luck with that mate!" another man joined in the debate. "The owners'll not spend a penny more'n they 'ave to no matter how many lives it costs us 'cos the old ways aint safe."

Joe listened in to the discussions raging around him; it seemed everyone had a different opinion. The more he thought about it the more confused he felt; at the end of the day the people in power, including the coal owners, were always going to win against the common workers.

"What d'you think Stan?" he turned to his friend sitting on his right. Stan was a man who considered things deeply and when he spoke people listened.

"Well, Joe, I think Churchill probably thinks he has the best of us. I hear he's got Baldwin to recruit more than 200,000 extra Special Constables so he must think there's gonna be some fight. They're being paid twice what us miners get for working down the pit so there'll be no shortage of volunteers, I reckon."

The area around them had fallen silent as men turned to hear what Stan Barlow had to say. One or two took a swallow of their beer, while the smoke from their cigarettes curled languidly upwards.

"But I guess he's not reckoned that they'll just be working for money while we'll be fighting for our lives; for our families and communities. If we lose this one lads, we might as well fasten the shackles around our own ankles; we'll never be free of the owners."

It was with a heavy heart that Joe tramped back down the hill towards home. Whatever happened next of one thing he was certain: the miners would face it together.

Of course, the women weren't invited to these meetings. Most men believed a woman's place was in the home, her mind struggling to cope with doing the washing and bringing up the kids. They refused to acknowledge that their lives would be much harder without a good woman behind them: cleaning their bodies and clothes, feeding them up and tending to every ailment so they were ready for the rigours of a mining life.

This meant nothing to the likes of Joe's sisters or indeed Jean Evans, who had never felt the need to ask a man's permission for anything. They knew who really kept things together when times were hard. Even now several such women were clustered together in Eva's kitchen discussing what the coming strike would mean to them and their families.

"I blames the government. 'Land fit for heroes' don't make me laugh. We all pitched in and did our bit and now they're leavin' us high and dry." Winnie Slater's anger and bitterness was understandable: she had lost two young sons to the war; now they lay somewhere on Flanders' fields. Her husband, Arthur, had been forced to take datal work at bank: he could hardly breathe thanks to more than thirty years working down the pits.

Ellen nodded her head, then spoke up, "Our Ginny reckons Churchill will be out to make a name for himself by stamping hard on any workers who come out on strike. it looks like he's already planning to call the forces out against us." She shivered involuntarily at the thoughts of their men facing trained soldiers on the picket lines. "But no matter what happens we've got to let them know we'll back them all the way. This isn't just about us but the futures of our kids and their bairns after them.

A general consensus of agreement ran around the room. "We're with you, girl." Winnie said, "Here Eva, you're educated, come and keep a record of what we need to do and of who will do what so's there'll be no arguin' later."

"Like minutes of the meeting, you mean?" Eva asked.

"Aye, that's right, lass. If we're gonna get organised proper like, we may as well do it right from the start."

By the time the women left to go home to finish preparing dinner for their families, they had allocated responsibilities amongst the group. Some would be enlisting volunteers from amongst the community; others would approach the Working Men's Club to allow them to set up a soup kitchen, as that would be where the miners would most likely meet during the dispute; more would draw up lists of who would be able to donate, not money, but food for strikers and their families. They all agreed that no matter what, the children would not go hungry.

Although Eva had known of several strikes in the mines around Wain Hill as she grew up, she had never felt their affects directly. She realised now just how sheltered had been her old life. Even as she studied the determination on the faces of the women now planning their defences, like generals going to war, she felt her baby kick strongly. It was a timely reminder that they were fighting to maintain dignity of labour; recognition for the cruel and dangerous work miners faced every day and for the futures of their sons and daughters.

CHAPTER THIRTY-ONE

As the end of April approached the owners put their cards on the table. When the subsidy ended the miners would face wage cuts between ten and twenty-five percent, while face workers hours would be extended from seven to eight hours per shift. Take it or leave it.

How could anyone expect a man, working in such a physically demanding and dangerous job like coal hewing, feed a family on £1-10s-3d a week. This was made worse by the fact that the extra two hundred and twenty-six thousand special constables the government had been recruiting in the previous nine months, were being paid £2-6s-3d.

The men refused to accept the pay cuts and on the first of May 1926 every miner in Britain downed tools and walked out. The owners locked the gates behind them and said no-one would be allowed back until they accepted the new conditions.

At first spirits were high. For men used to hard physical work, a few extra days off were more than welcome. Bella, Eva now being very near her time, had come to stay for the duration. Joe, as much to get out from under the women's feet as anything, decided to take a walk up to Jack's. They could always spend a couple of hours at the allotment; there was plenty that needed seeing to there, especially as they had planted more vegetables than was usual; they would be much needed if the strike continued for any length of time.

Walking straight in through the back door, he found Ellen up to her armpits in washing and babies. "Have you come to give us a hand then, our Joe," Ellen laughed, "or are you after that husband of mine?" The room was over-warm and filled with steam, the fire built up to ensure a good supply of hot water.

"Aye, I thowt we might take a walk up the allotment."

"He's ahead of you there! He beat a hasty retreat as soon as I pulled the wash tub out, but at least he took Alice with him; although I dread to think what state he'll bring her back in." Her daughter's fondness for making mud pies had led to one or two arguments in the past.

Joe grinned at the thought of his niece up to the eyes in mud. "I've left Eva and Bella to it as well. Us husbands know when we're not wanted." He tried to look crestfallen but the twinkle in his eyes gave him away. "I'll follow him up, then. With a bit of luck he'll have the kettle on. There's no chance of getting' a cup of tea when you women get started on your washin'." He ducked to avoid the wet towel his sister skilfully threw at him.

"Get out of here and don't come back 'til dinner time!"

The sun shone warm on his back as Joe made his way up the narrow path towards Paradise Gardens. Many miners had obviously had the same thoughts as himself, in nearly every garden there was a man hard at work digging, planting or weeding his growing crops. Many hailed him by name as he passed, whistling merrily. It was times like these he realised how much he missed the old days with Ginny on the small holding; it wasn't just Eva who had had to get used to a new way life.

Looking back over Essingham, he could see numerous small boats out on the sea; some would be lifting lobster pots, others would be fishing for the table. Maybe he should see Fred, get him to take him out in his boat; there was nothing tastier than a bit of fresh cod.

It was strange to see the pit standing idle; no clamour from the yard; no clang of rolling stock; no wheels turning over the shafts. The officials would still be at work making sure the workings stayed safe until the men's return but there could be no production without miners to man the coal-cutting machines or the hundred and one other jobs that went into securing the black gold.

As soon as he opened the gate, Alice ran into his waiting arms. He swung her round high in the air, laughing and giggling, screaming, "More Uncle Joe! More!". She staggered around dizzily when he finally deposited her back on the garden path. "Come and help me look for worms, Uncle Joe." She held tightly to his fingers, pulling him towards the bare patch of earth where she had been digging.

"Let Uncle Joe abee Missy. And don't you get any more mud on you than you have to or I'll have your Mam after me." Jack straightened from where he had been planting cabbages in one of the beds. He turned his attention to his brother-in-law. "I wondered when you would turn up. Eva let you have a lie-in or summat?"

Joe laughed making his way towards the shed at one end of the hen-house. "Any water left in the kettle? Oh, and don't let me forget to take some eggs back; Bella's partial to a boiled egg for breakfast."

Joe made the tea in large white mugs and carried them out to where two old wooden chairs were placed to catch the sun. Jack joined him and they sat in silence for a while watching Alice as she continued her worm-hunt.

"How long d'you reckon we'll be out then?" Joe asked.

"Dunno, hopefully no more than a couple of weeks now they know we mean business. Depends if we can get anyone else out to support us, I suppose." Jack hoped he sounded more convincing than he felt; he knew Joe was worried, especially with Eva being so near her time. "We can only hope the government puts some pressure on the owners to do the right thing."

Sitting there in the sunshine, it was hard to think too long on what the consequences of a lengthy strike might be. What was that Ginny always said? Que sera sera.

The TUC met urgently with the government to try to find some agreement but were sorely disappointed when the government backed, not the miners, but the coal owners. The owners were adamant that their final deal already lay on the table. Faced with such determination, the TUC had little choice but to call on all of its members to strike in support of the miners. On the fourth of May, to a man, everyone downed tools in the first organised General Strike.

Joe, having been in the crowd of miners standing

outside the pit gates for want of something better to do, when the news came through, cheered as loudly as anyone. Surely now the government would have to intervene. He couldn't wait to get back home to tell Eva and Bella.

If he had expected them to jump up and down with excitement, then he was sorely disappointed. "Don't you see?" he implored them, "the government can't let the whole country come out. They'll have to do summat now."

"Yes Joe, " Bella responded, " but it might not be in the way we would all like. If they can persuade enough people that the miners are as much of a threat as the reds in Russia, then who knows how they will react. They may even call out the army."

This stopped Joe in his tracks; surely no-one could ever think that the miners wanted to overthrow the government.

"Not only that, but when all those people living in the towns and cities have to face a life without any transport, or when they can't buy what they like in the shops, how many of them are going to care about some miners living out in the sticks? I'm sorry Joe, but when it comes down to it people are generally a selfish bunch."

Joe felt he'd had the wind driven right out of his

sails but he knew in his heart what Bella had said was true. As in the past, it would be up to the miners to make a stand for the rights of workers to a fair day's pay for their labours.

At first it seemed as if Bella would be proved wrong. Production of all the national newspapers had ceased but Joe managed to pick up a copy of The British Worker, produced by the TUC. They reported that the national transport system had ground to a standstill and that strikers had total control over the transport of goods around the country or coming into docks. The triple alliance was holding strong and many other unions were coming out in support of the miners.

In coalfields throughout Britain, men raised their glasses to the success of the strike. In the face of such solidarity, surely the government would not only have to listen to their grievances but to act accordingly.

The government did react, but not as they had hoped. Churchill oversaw the publishing of a government newspaper, The British Gazette. Joe and his friends listened in dismay as its front page was read out by one of the Federation's officials. The miners were not only being castigated as trouble makers but were being painted as traitorous revolutionaries whose only aim was to destroy

Baldwin's government.

Moreover, it seemed the government had also been busy in the months before the strike recruiting an army of volunteers whose names were listed by the Organisation of Maintenance of Supplies. Thousands of people who felt no affiliation with the workers' struggle, chiefly from amongst the Middle Classes in the South, from University students looking for a bit of adventure and from the unemployed, flocked to sign up to this venture. They manned the buses, unloaded cargoes and drove lorries, which greatly lessened the effects of the strike.

The army, navy and police were brought in to guard the docks, telephone exchanges and power stations and this show of military might, scared many into returning to work. The whole of the United Kingdom was divided up into ten areas each controlled by a member of the government. The country was being placed in a state of emergency under martial law.

A deathly silence fell over the room; no-one could believe their ears. Then someone at the back shouted out: 'Not a penny off the pay; not a minute on the day'. Suddenly there was pandemonium as hundreds of men expressed their anger at being betrayed by their own government.

No-one was surprised when only days later, the TUC, afraid of losing public opinion and a mass return to work by their members, caved in and called off the strike.

Once more the miners were on their own, but they were more determined than ever.

CHAPTER THIRTY-TWO

In bed, Eva tossed and turned restlessly. No matter which way she lay, she could not get comfortable: her back ached. Joe snored softly beside her. It was nice having him there all of the time without the constant worry of the pit hanging over their heads. Rock falls, gas, machinery; the other women seemed armoured against such everyday dangers, but, unused to having to live with them constantly there in the back of her mind, Eva feared for Joe every time he went down into that black hole.

She wondered what the time was. Perhaps she'd get up and make herself a cup of tea; with luck the fire would still be on. Ungainly due to the huge bump she now carried before her, she rolled to the side of the bed to swing her legs down onto the floor. A pain stopped her in her tracks; it only lasted a few seconds so that she questioned whether she'd really felt it at all. Perhaps it was wind. Joe slept on, oblivious.

The kitchen was still warm; the clock on the mantel told her it was two o'clock. She didn't bother with a light; the curtains remained open and moonlight flooded the room. Stirring life back into the glowing embers, she moved the filled kettle further onto the coals to boil and settled back onto her chair, placing a cushion behind her aching back.

This time the pain was more definite: she could feel her muscles tightening as the contraction took hold. It was not yet strong enough to cause her any real discomfort. Later the real pain would begin; it could be a long night. It would be nice to sit alone there for a while in the welcome stillness of the kitchen to await the birth of her baby.

She must have dozed for a while, because when she awoke the kettle was boiling furiously. She struggled forward and used the oven cloth to lift it off the fire, carefully pouring the boiling liquid onto the leaves ready in the teapot. She rose with difficulty and fetched herself a cup and saucer from the dresser. On her way to retrieve the milk from the cold shelf in the scullery, the next pain took her, much stronger this time so that she caught hold of the edge of the table and steadied herself until it passed. She was relieved when she made it back to her chair. She would have her tea then wake the others. There was time enough.

The kitchen door opened, and her mother came into the room wearing a rose-pink dressing gown over her nightdress, her hair loose about her shoulders. "I thought I heard someone down here. Can't sleep, darling?"

"I think the baby's coming Mam."

Bella wanted to run to her but instead she took a deep breath; it was not in her nature to panic: it helped no-one. "Are you sure? How long in between the pains?"

"Don't worry, Mam, it's a long way off yet; they seem to be coming every fifteen minutes or so but they are getting stronger. Do you think we should wake Joe?"

"No, love, let him sleep. Men are best off out of the way at times like these. Do you think you'll be able to manage some breakfast? You're going to need your strength, you know."

Eva smiled. "Do you think I could have a soft-boiled egg with soldiers? The way you used to make them when I was little?"

Bella stroked Eva's hair away from her face, "Of course, my love. Just you rest there. I'll even get Joe's breakfast on the go too; there's nothing much stops his appetite, now is there?"

When Joe woke he was surprised to find that Eva was not beside him. He leapt out of bed, pulled on some pants and hurried downstairs. It wasn't often that the two women beat him out of bed on a morning. "What's gannin' on here, then?" he asked. "Is this a private party or can anyone join in?"

"Oh, nothing much," Eva replied, "I'm only having the baby that's all."

"Should I away and fetch Mrs. Hailes then?" Joe looked about ready to run from the house dressed only in his pants.

"No need for that yet, Joe," Bella told him, "Why don't you sit yourself down and eat this fine breakfast I've made you. Mind don't expect me to do it every morning. You're big enough and ugly enough to feed yourself."

By the time Joe had finished his meal and made himself presentable, Eva's contractions were coming only five minutes apart. Joe sat by her side, holding her hand, not even wincing when she gripped his fingers tightly as the pains grew in their ferocity. Now the initial shock had passed he was much more in control; after all he had grown up helping many an animal into this world. At last Bella agreed that it was time for him to fetch Mrs. Hailes.

"Joe," Eva shouted him as he was going out of the door, "could you run and ask Ellen to come too, please?" She really wanted her sister-in-law to share in the birth of this baby. Ellen was the sister she had never had growing up, and their babies would bring them even closer together.

"Oh, and Joe, "Bella interceded, "could you call at the phone box on the way back and call Thomas and let him know what's happening, please?"

Joe felt like a schoolboy being sent out to do errands. "Is there owt else?" The two women simply shook their heads and he was off like a whippet out of the traps.

When Joe reached Ellen's, she was alone in the house with the children. It looked as if he would have to baby sit until Jack got back off the picket line. Despite Joe's protests, Ellen assured him that he would be best off out of it; having babies was most definitely women's work.

"There's a pan of broth on the fire; it'll be ready by the time Jack's back so's you and him can get a dish of that for your dinners. If you need owt else then knock on the fireback for Jean and she'll be straight in. Don't look so worried Joe, Eva's in good hands. It'll all be over afore you know it."

Alice, wise beyond her years perhaps, came over to take Joe's hand. "C'mon Uncle Joe, you can practise puttin' nappies on my dolly, if you like." What else could Joe do but laugh?

By the time Ellen got to Eva's, Mrs. Hailes had

everything in hand. Eva had been put to bed, protective layers of newspaper and draw sheets beneath her. Her contractions were now coming every couple of minutes but her waters had not yet broken. That was how Mrs. Hailes, 'call me Molly', liked it, she told Bella; while the sac remained intact there was less risk of infection. Bella had to admit this kindly lady seemed to know exactly what she was doing.

Eva lay back on her pillows, her fair hair darkened and her face flushed with perspiration. She had never felt such pain as this in her entire life; but she did not complain. Molly was using a trumpet-like instrument to listen to the baby's heart through Eva's abdomen.

"That's a good lass," Molly said, "Save all your strength, lovey. I'm gonna break your waters now pet, it's time to get this baby moving."

Eva felt a sudden release as Molly ruptured the sac and the amniotic fluid gushed out onto the bed. "Right you two, get these wet covers off and dry ones on, quick as you like now."

Ellen and Bella rolled the sodden sheets into a bundle which Ellen took straight down and threw onto the fire. A clean layer of paper and sheet soon replaced them. Just in time as Eva's next contraction came hard and fast.

"Now don't push Eva, just pant like mad, this baby's in an almighty rush to be born now but it'll have to wait a minute more." Molly expertly guided the head turning it carefully so that the nose and mouth were exposed to the air. Eva was thankful that she had attended Ellen's labour, for now she knew exactly what was happening.

"Right Eva, when the next pain comes I want you to push as hard as you can. Ready? Now push!"

Eva held her breath and bore down with every ounce of strength she had and, with very little help from Molly, her baby slid smoothly out into the world.

"You have a boy," her mother shouted, "a beautiful baby boy!"

Laughing and crying at once, Eva watched as Molly cleared her son's airways of mucus and cut and tied the cord, before wrapping him in a towel and handing him to her. She pulled back the cover to gaze at him; he was perfect in every way.

The peace was shattered when Joe burst into the kitchen, ran through the front parlour and took the stairs two at a time. The bedroom door flung open and he erupted into the room. The women moved back far enough to allow him to see Eva cradling his son.

"Hello Joe," Eva smiled, "Meet Tommy. Tommy this is your Dad, the best husband in the world."

"Well go on then," Molly Hailes piped up, "Give your wife and son a kiss then pass him over so's I can weigh him."

It was enough to break the spell and all at once everyone was talking and laughing. Joe gave Eva a smacking kiss then gently took his son in his arms for the first time at which point Tommy decided to let everyone hear how loudly he could scream. Joe thankfully passed him over into Molly's capable hands.

Turning back to the bed he asked, "Is there anything you want Eva? Anything at all?" He looked at his wife with loving eyes.

"Ee Joe I'd kill for a cup of tea!"

Joe was shooed out of the room. The baby may have been born but the birth was a long way from over. Molly Hailes would only be happy when the afterbirth was out and complete. Then the women could make Eva comfortable whilst she bathed the baby. Eva was lucky to have such good support to help her through these first few strange weeks as she and her son got to know each other. Not all the miners' wives were so fortunate.

CHAPTER THIRTY-THREE

Six weeks into the strike spirits remained high. The weather was warm and most had managed to save towards surviving with no wages; the vast majority of men were standing firm. Those few who returned to work were vilified by their fellow miners. Each morning they had to cross the picket line outside the pit gates where strikers gathered to form a picket line. 'Scab!' 'Yer ought to be ashamed of yersel'' rang in their ears as they hurried past, heads down against the onslaught of verbal abuse.

Special Constables linked arms, forming a barrier in front of the protesters, to protect those crossing the lines from actual violence. Most of these 'policemen' came from outside the area but not all. There would be several held to account after the strike.

Joe, had always regarded his height an advantage; he had been proud to stand head and sometimes shoulders above the rest of his fellow miners. Now, however, he found he was always one of the first to be targeted for attention; there were one or two of the Specials who enjoyed taking advantage of the safety of being in a group, who made sure they were stationed opposite him when he was on the line.

One Wednesday morning, Joe was manning the picket line with thirty or forty of his workmates, when the Specials formed their cordon in front of them. He almost choked when he looked up and found himself face to face with Ned Sherringham. He knew Ned was a nasty piece of work but he had never imagined he would stoop so low. He longed to reach out and wipe the smug smirk off the other man's face. Ned's eyes glittered with contempt.

"Not so big now, are you Fishburn?" he snarled. "You better watch your step 'cos I'll be waitin' for you." The hatred poured out of him; they'd refused to allow him down the pit with the other deputies; he wasn't qualified yet, didn't have his tickets, so he'd enlisted as a Special Constable. He felt good in his uniform and the pay was far more than any of them would ever earn. Now he was hoping that the strikers would overstep the mark and give him the opportunity to cave Joe Fishburn's head in with his night stick.

Joe gritted his teeth; it would be a big mistake to say what he was thinking aloud. As the bus carrying the scabs pulled up, the mood of the strikers shifted. As one they surged forwards to shake fists and hurl abuse at these men who had betrayed them. Joe almost allowed himself to be pushed into the police line, but thoughts of Eva and his new born son held him back. He let the others absorb him back into the crowd where Ned could not reach him.

Afterwards, the incident left a bitter taste in Joe's mouth; never before had he been afraid of another man. But now he had a wife and baby at home; they were his number one priority. Once the strike breakers were safely inside the pit yard, the men began to disperse. A few would be left to try to ensure that no goods made it into or out of the pit. Joe looked around for his mate, Stan. He needed to talk.

He found him with a group of older men, planning tactics. One look at Joe's face told Stan that his friend was extremely worried about something. They walked off to the side, away from prying ears, and Joe told him about what had happened.

"A think it would be best if you didn't gan on the line anymore, Joe."

"I can't let him see he's got the better of me, Stan. We've all got to do our bit; he doesn't scare me!" But he did scare him; not for himself but for Eva and Tommy. What would they do if anything happened to him?

"It's not a case of being scared, bonny lad, but we've got to be sensible. If he starts layin' into you the whole place'll gan up; it's hard enough tryin' to keep some of the young'uns in check as it is.

They'd just love the excuse to get stuck into those scabs and the Specials.

"You leave Ned to us. It's his poor parents I feel for: one son lost in the war and now the other turned traitor against his own; they must be devastated."

Joe could see the sense in Stan's words but it didn't make him feel any better about the situation. Stan put a comforting arm around Joe's shoulder. "Divn't worry there's plenty of other ways you can be of use. We'll have a chat with the committee and see what's to be done."

When he got home, Joe found Eva sitting in her chair feeding Tommy. The sight of his son at his wife's breast filled him with so much love. Who could hold on to anger in the face of such a perfect picture? He crossed the room and kissed her tenderly on the lips.

"How was it this morning, love? Has there any more gone back?"

"One or two, I reckon," he replied, although he would tell her nothing of what had happened. "You know Eva, I could almost feel sorry for some of them."

Eva looked up in surprise but waited for him to

continue.

"Some of them looked scared to death. Why do they do it? I thought; why face that every day? And then I could see that some of them are just family men doing the best they know how to look after their wife and kids."

It was Joe's turn to be surprised when Eva countered, "Yes, well it's a pity they didn't think more of them earlier then and saved against the hard times. We all knew this strike was going to come off long before it did. But it didn't stop some of these 'family men' pouring beer down their throats or squandering their wages on pitch and toss or the horses."

Joe blinked; it was unlike Eva to erupt in this way and it seemed she wasn't finished yet.

"A lot of the women blame the scabs' wives for nagging them back to work instead of making do with what they've got like the rest of us. They're so short sighted they can't see that it's not just our livelihood we're fighting for but for the futures of our children, like little Tommy here, and our children's children!"

Tommy, unused to his mother's ire, left off her breast and began to cry. Eva lifted him up onto her shoulder and patted his back to bring up the wind.

"Don't you waste too much of your sympathy on the likes of them, Joe. They made their bed so let them lie in it. Now, lift that pie crust out of the oven before it's burned to a crisp."

Joe looked at his wife with new eyes. Gone was the girl, her place taken by this strong woman who, in such a short time, had become a capable, loving wife and born him a healthy, handsome son. Whistling softly, he gladly set the table ready for their dinner.

CHAPTER THIRTY-FOUR

Thomas strode briskly down Church Street, enjoying the early morning sunshine. Things may not be going so well in his business but whose spirits could not be lifted by being alive on such a beautiful Summer's morning. Bella had placed him on a new fitness regime, of which the extra exercise of walking to work was a part. Meals were also a much simpler affair these days; it was hard to justify eating so well when many in their community had to do without. Besides, Bella said that it would do neither of them any harm to lose a bit of weight.

Letting himself into the shop, he paused to look around. Master of all he surveyed, he smiled to himself. It was a long way from Stewart Street where he had been brought up. Sighing, he hung his jacket up behind the door in the back shop and donned a clean white apron. The baker would be delivering his bread soon, although the order would be greatly diminished: few could afford shop-bought bread let alone cakes these days. It would be good when the strike was over and things could get back to normal.

The bell dinged loudly and he returned to the front shop to check on his visitor but it was only Roland.

He had had to let his staff go when the strike began to bite but he still had his son, and sometimes Bella to help in the shop. Everyone had to do their bit.

"Morning Dad," Roland was looking decidedly sheepish.

"And what, may I ask, happened to you last night, young man?" It was obvious that Roland had not slept at home from the pristine state of his bed that morning.

"Sorry, I stayed over at Frank's. I should have told you I might. A few of us got together, played some records and chatted. When I realised the time, it was too late to go out and find a phone box."

"Hmm. Your mother was worried." Although he must admit it had perturbed him much more than Bella to think their son had stayed out all night again. It was happening far too often lately.

Roland smiled weakly. If his father only knew where he really was there'd be Hell to pay. He had spent the evening with friends, it was true, but they had been over the pit heap scavenging coal waste. The July evenings might be warm enough but everyone still needed their fires for cooking and to heat water. The discarded coal dust or 'duff' as it was known, made good fuel when compacted into 'bricks'.

The July days being so long, the lads had to wait until one or two in the morning for enough darkness to obscure their activities. Sometimes the army sent soldiers to patrol the pit heaps but up until now the look-outs had done their job and given them enough warning for them to make their escape. He had to admit he found the whole thing rather exciting but it would never do for the Church Warden's son to be brought up for stealing!

Thomas wasn't totally convinced but he decided to let the matter drop. After all Roland was twenty-four, more than old enough to look after himself. He'd like to think that one day he might get serious about one of the young girls he cavorted with and settle down.

Roland made himself busy, sorting out any fruit and vegetables that were on the turn and putting them to one side. They were still good enough to go into the communal pots in the soup kitchen at the Church Hall. Desperate to get back into his father's good books he suggested, "Why don't you and Mam have a ride over to see our Eva and the baby for a bit? I can manage here; it's not as if we'll be rushed off our feet on a Wednesday."

Thomas brightened at once. It would be nice to see his grandson, and his daughter too, of course. He had been so proud when they had named their firstborn Thomas. He could take Eva one or two things; nothing too much, maybe a bag of flour and a bit of butter. She needed to keep her strength up while she was feeding the baby. Perhaps a few sherbet lemons as well; she'd always been fond of a sherbet lemon.

He'd sort out the food vouchers that had come in last week and drop them off at the Union. He'd probably have to wait a week or two for the money but at least the men couldn't spend them on beer or gambling; although he could think of one or two that might try.

Bella would probably be at the Church Hall helping out in the soup kitchen; he'd collect her on the way home, grab a bite to eat, then head over to Essingham. Maybe a couple of slices of bacon would be welcome too.

Eva was not at home; she was up at Ellen's making meat and tatie pies. Jean Evans and one or two other neighbours had joined them. They were part of the small army of women who were churning out three meals a day for four hundred school children funded by the local Labour Council.

Freddy and Tommy were tucked up in their prams outside in the sunshine where Ellen and Eva could keep an eye on them through the window. Both doors, front and back, were propped open to let what little breeze there was blow through the crowded room.

The kitchen was steaming hot; large pans of potatoes were boiling on the fire while great dishes of mincemeat were cooking in the range oven. Later, when the pies were ready to be baked, it would get even hotter; it needed a very hot oven to brown pastry.

The women, wrapped in their pinnies, hair protected by headsquare turbans, peeled and chopped, sliced and measured; all the while keeping up a steady stream of banter, sometimes bursting spontaneously into song.

By eleven o'clock, there were dozens of large golden pies packed ready and waiting on the table. They might be more tatie than meat, Eva thought, but the children wouldn't mind that; at least they would be filling and smothered in mushy peas they would be tasty too. They had steeped the peas in buckets the night before then boiled them in the biggest pans they could find on several of the neighbours' fires. Ellen hoped the men wouldn't be long or they would be cold again before they got them to the school.

Right on cue, Joe pulled up in a horse and cart in

the back lane. The other men with him soon had the cart loaded. Three more women emerged from gates further down the street and climbed up onto the back of the cart; they would help to distribute the food and bring back any utensils once the children had been fed. There might only be porridge for breakfast and jam'n'bread for tea but at least they wouldn't starve.

Joe jumped down and gave Eva a quick kiss. "I hope you've saved a couple of those pies for me dinner, pet. It's hungry work cartin' this lot about y'know."

"Get away with you, you're loving it. It must feel like old times."

"Aye, old Whitey here isn't Samson but he's willing enough. It's good to feel the reins again. I'll drop this lot off then see you back home, love."

"I'll be a while yet, Joe," Eva replied, "We're making a batch of stotties while the oven's hot so I'll be a couple of hours at least. Don't you dare touch anything in that pantry before I get home!"

Joe grinned in reply; as if he would do such a thing!

It was good to see Joe smiling, Eva thought, back to his old self instead of worrying about how they would manage from day to day. They were the lucky ones; there was plenty of fresh veg from the allotment and the hens were still laying well. True, there wasn't so much in the way of meat but Fred sometimes dropped them off a fish, and Joe had been rabbiting with a couple of the other lads once or twice. And, despite Joe's protestations, her Dad never came empty handed. They would survive.

An hour later, when Joe got home, he found Thomas and Bella waiting in their car outside his house.

"Thank goodness you're back, Joe." Bella said as she got out of the vehicle. "We were just about to go up to your Ellen's to look for Eva."

"And you'd have found her," Joe laughed. "The women have been bakin' for the kids' meals all mornin'. It's like a bakery up there. Are you comin' in for a cuppa then?"

"Is Tommy up there with her?" Thomas asked. He had been disappointed not to find his grandson at home, "Only we can't stay too long: Roland's alone in the shop and I'd like to get back before closing."

"Where else? Why don't you go up and take him a walk in his pram? It's a shame to be in on a day like this."

Thomas looked distinctly uncomfortable as he said,

"I've just got one or two things to drop off, for our Eva and the baby like; will you take them?"

Joe's eyes flashed. "You know we can manage, Tom. I can still fend for us!"

"We know you can, Joe, and always will but being able to help a little makes us feel better too." Bella intervened gently, "Eva doesn't stop being our daughter just because she's your wife, and Tommy is our grandson after all." She smiled as she continued, "And you don't have to eat it, after all."

Joe couldn't stop his answering smile. He knew he was being unreasonable, "Give us it here, then."

Bella and Thomas spent a pleasant afternoon wheeling their grandson up Seaside Lane in his pram like the proud grandparents they were. Thomas couldn't resist calling in at the local grocer's for a chat about business and Bella bought a beautiful white suit for Tommy at Sherburn Hill Co-operative Store. By the time they got back to Court Street, Eva was back from Ellen's and had the kettle boiling on the fire. They only stayed for a quick cup as Thomas was anxious to get back to his shop. Joe and Eva saw them away; Eva lifting the baby's arm to wave as they drove away. She felt a little nostalgic for the days before she was a wife and mother but she would not have gone back for anything.

CHAPTER THIRTY-FIVE

The Summer of '26 was long and hot. The men were determined to make the best of it; more used to spending their days in the dark, the fine weather and long Summer evenings were most welcome. They had never looked fitter or healthier as their skins turned golden in the sun.

Many filled their hours by foraging for food in the nearby countryside; farmers often turning a blind eye if several bare patches appeared amongst their vegetable crops. Likewise, the local gamekeeper was not quite as vigilant these days; as long as no-one went after his game birds, a few rabbits poached for the pot would make little inroad into their numbers. Down on the beach, while men cast out their fishing lines, the women and children gathered mussels from the rocks.

One of the main events was an organised football match between the men and the women to take place on the football ground in the Welfare Park late in August. Essingham was proud of its football team: they had been league Champions for the last two years. Of course, none of the first team would be allowed to play against the women, it did not seem fair, but there were plenty of other lads who fancied themselves as great players.

This was closely matched by the rivalry amongst the women to be selected for their team. Normally excluded from this male-only world, they were only too eager to pit their skills against the men. They bragged that what they lacked in muscle, they more than made up for in brains and speed. Their most pressing problem was finding enough appropriate kit. Although several women already possessed shorts, none had suitable shirts, much less football boots. This was remedied when some of the older schoolboys volunteered, with a little persuasion from their mothers, to donate their own strips.

A couple of brave men stepped forward to act as managers for the women's team; it would be their job to teach them the rules and go over possible tactics. The women were so determined, they met up for several training sessions in the week before the match. In mis-matched uniforms and ill-fitting boots they may have been a rag-tag band but none could doubt their ferocity as they charged up and down the field after the ball.

A crowd of young men gathered to observe these sessions. At first they jeered and shouted at the women but by the end of the week most gained a healthy respect for these gritty girls. Soon their jeers turned to cheers whenever one of the women scored a goal.

The day of the match dawned fair. People came from miles around to watch the spectacle. Men and women, young and old, children of all ages, gathered in the Welfare Park, bringing with them blankets and picnic baskets; everyone determined to enjoy the day to the full. The only sour note was the numbers of Special Constables in evidence, lining the edges of the roads and field; supposedly there to keep the peace.

Bella and Thomas had brought Ginny over to join in the fun. Joe and Jack would both be playing on the men's team, although Joe had to profess football had never really been his game. Ellen and Eva laid a large tartan blanket on the grass at the far end of the field where several trees afforded some shade for the babies. Everyone tucked into the pies and stottie sandwiches the women had made, waiting for the match to begin.

At five to three the brave referee walked out to the middle of the pitch and called for both teams to take their places. The men and women greeted each other warmly, shaking hands and laughing as they wished each other the best of luck. There were eleven players on each side but numerous substitutes stood ready on the sidelines, hoping to be called on to play.

At three o'clock precisely, the referee blew his

whistle and Peggy Holcroft, the women's Captain, kicked off. As expected the men charged at the women, but to give the women their due, they were not intimidated. Several of the larger women guarded the smaller ones from the men's challenges, allowing them to neatly side-step them and speed towards the goal.

The battle was fierce; the action moving swiftly from one end of the ground to the other. The crowds were jumping up and down and cheering both sides on. But, by half-time, the men were winning by six goals to two. It was hardly surprising; the women knew little about maintaining their positions or marking opposition players. Several had already gone off injured: not all of the men played fair!

Both teams mustered on the sidelines for much needed drinks and team talks. While the men were obviously congratulating themselves, the women were huddled in deep discussion. Ten minutes later, everyone was back on the field and the whistle blew for the second half.

No-one quite knew how they managed it but suddenly the women were running for the goal and the keeper, caught cleverly off guard by two of the ladies, could only watch helplessly as the ball sailed past him into the back of the net. "Goal!" The crowd went wild.

The women were gaining on the men; they seemed to be everywhere at once. The ref's whistle blew shrilly, halting the players in their tracks. It seemed the women had managed to sneak an extra three players onto the pitch without anyone on the men's team noticing. The men were indignant; why hadn't they thought of that?

After much good-humoured shouting on both sides, the match resumed. The men finally running out easy victors. Even some of the Specials clapped as the teams left the field. Joe and Jack muddied and sweaty made their way over to where the rest of their family was standing. The women were busy picking up plates and cups and folding the blanket before packing everything onto the tray under Tommy's pram.

Thomas, in his shirt sleeves for once, was holding Tommy, jiggling him up and down in the air so that he laughed and giggled. "Best game of football I've ever seen," he said as the boys drew nearer. "I haven't laughed so much in a long time."

Joe took his son from him. "A reckon my shins are bruised to bits, Tom. Those women don't fight fair, I can tell you."

"Don't be such a baby!" Eva mocked him. "Big strong brutes like you, taking on poor little women; you should feel ashamed of yourselves."

"It's a good job you weren't playin' love, or we wouldn't have stood a chance."

Everyone agreed they had had a grand day. For a few short hours, all worries about the strike had been put behind them. The only cloud came as they were leaving the park. Off to one side, Joe saw Ned Sherringham watching him and his family as they walked by. His look was not a friendly one.

CHAPTER THIRTY-SIX

As Summer waned and days grew shorter, more and more families found it harder to cope. Allotments were stripped bare and where food and funds had once poured in from outside, the colliery communities were forced more and more to rely totally on their own resources. Clothes and shoes continually handed down, were now beginning to wear out completely, with no money left to buy replacements.

Ironically in villages built out of coal, the cold was now an enemy. The pit heaps were more closely guarded by Specials and troops but many ventured down the railway lines, where duff could still be found in the embankments. It was a precarious task, however; you couldn't dig in very far without the risk of being buried alive when the overhang gave way.

Late in September, Eva and Joe had decided to take a walk along the beach banks towards Hawthorne. They had often come this way when they were courting and the late Summer sunshine would help them to forget their worries for an hour or two.

Pushing the pram before them, they crossed under the railway bridge and were just about to cut down past East allotments, when a young lad come tearing down one of the side paths towards them. He was covered from head to toe in coal dust; white streaks ran down his face where he kept wiping away a stream of tears. His face was twisted in horror.

"Mister, Mister," he yelled when he saw Joe, "Yer've gotta come; Jimmy's buried in the bank."

Joe, at once grasping the truth of the situation turned to Eva, "Get back to the yard and tell some of the men to come quick; a young lad's got himself buried under the embankment."

Turning the pram, Eva was almost running back the way they had come; it wasn't easy pushing the pram over the rough paths but a young lad's life may depend on her getting help quickly.

"Right lad, show me where your mate is!"

The boy didn't need bidding twice; he turned and ran back down the path closely followed by Joe. It took them several minutes to make it through the gardens and a couple of hundred yards further along the black path, past the pitch and toss clearing. Where normally they could hope to find several men hanging about watching the game, it was deserted; no-one had the wherewithal these days for gambling.

Beyond this, Joe could see a dark scar where the embankment had given way exposing fresh black duff. There was no sign of the other boy only a discarded spade thrown to one side.

"He's in there Mister," the lad said, pointing towards the mound at the base of the slippage. "I told him we was in too far but he wouldn't listen."

Joe raced to the bank, picked up the spade and began digging for all he was worth. Time was against them: if the lad hadn't been crushed by the weight of the duff, then he would probably suffocate. Pausing, he shouted, "Jimmy, Jimmy we're coming to get you," although he knew there was little likelihood that the boy could hear him.

He turned back to his friend, "Run back to where you found me and wait for the others and bring them here as fast as you can." The boy just stood there, shaking so hard his teeth were rattling. "Go on, I'll get your marra out." The boy took off. Joe knew the chances of finding the lad alive were slim and he didn't want the other boy there. There were some things a young'un should never have to face.

As he turned to sink the spade once more into the earth, he caught sight of a black coat hurrying along the path from the opposite direction. His heart sank as he recognised Ned Sherringham.

"Now I've got you Fishburn!" Ned shouted, his face alight with glee, "They'll throw the book at you for stealin' coal and endangering the safety of the railway."

"Don't be daft, Ned. there's a young lad buried somewhere under this lot. For God's sake man come and give us a hand, will ya?"

The smile dropped from Ned's face; he didn't know whether to believe his old adversary or not. "A young lad, you say?"

"Aye, come on man every second counts!"

Ned imagined his older brother, Seth, standing beside him. 'What you waitin' for Ned,? You know what must be done, lad.' The vision faded.

Ned stripped off his heavy coat and looked round for something, anything he could use to help Joe dig. To one side stood a metal pail the lads had been filling with duff; he grabbed it and started plunging it frantically into the dirt of the embankment, scooping out great clods of earth. Together the men laboured on, battling against the odds; sweat streaming down their faces.

At last Joe revealed a foot clad in a worn, leather boot. "Steady now Ned, we don't want to risk hurting the lad. It's alright son, we've got you now." He couldn't be sure but he thought he saw the foot twitch.

Slowly, they peeled away the earth from around the young body, layer by layer. They were nearly there but then dirt began trickling from the overhang above their heads. "We need something to shore the roof," Joe said, "I wish the others would hurry up and get here. Ned, go and see if you can find summat we can wedge it with."

"No Joe, I can get further into the hole than you; you go, I'll stay here." Joe wanted to argue but he could see the sense in what Ned was saying: the smaller man could get further in to protect the boy than he could.

"I think I saw some old planks they've been using for seats by the pitch and toss. Just try not to dislodge any more dirt; I'll be as quick as I can."

Stooping over the boy, Ned continued to clear the muck from around the lad's nose and mouth. He slapped him hard on the back and he began to cough and splutter. Thank God! "Steady lad, don't worry we'll soon have you out. Do you think ye can wriggle back? That's it, easy now, nice and slow."

Ned could feel the dirt trickling down inside the neck of his shirt but the boy was almost clear now. He could hear men's voices and Joe's answering shout. The roof was dropping, weighing heavy on his back now. But the lad was safe; that's all that mattered. Somewhere the earth rumbled; he was falling, plunging into the darkness. Seth was there, smiling, welcoming him home.

Joe and the men broke into a run when they heard a deep rumble as the earth collapsed into the hole; a dust cloud obscured the entrance for a moment. The boy lay outside the hole gasping for breath. There was no sign of Ned.

It took them two hours to retrieve Ned's body from its earthen grave. Someone brought a door from one of the allotments and taking one end, Joe helped to carry him home. His parents were devastated.

One week later it seemed the whole of Essingham was in mourning, as men, women and children, dressed respectfully in black, lined Station Road as Ned's coffin was carried past on the Co-op's Hearse pulled by two black horses; ebony plumes on their headgear nodding solemnly as they trudged up the hill to the Church of the Ascension.

Although many had found cause to curse him when he was alive, in sacrificing his own life to save that of the young lad, Ned had redeemed himself in their eyes. His elderly parents may be immersed in their grief at his loss but at least now they could feel proud of both their sons.

CHAPTER THIRTY-SEVEN

Jack and Joe trudged wearily down the hill from their Paradise allotment. In a hessian sack they carried the last of the leeks and parsnips, and an old hen that had stopped laying and would serve them better now in the pot. The few men they passed on their way, hardly bothered to raise a hand in greeting. No-one had anything to smile about, Joe thought.

It looked like they would all be back at work by next week. 'Not a minute on the day, not a penny off the pay' their leaders had promised, but now they were to return to working longer hours for less wages. Defeat was a bitter pill to swallow. The owners had refused to give an inch and with the government behind them they had won the day.

The men of the Durham coalfields held out longer than most. Those in Nottingham and Derbyshire had returned by the end of August. But by November, months of existence on nothing but meagre lockout payments and charity took their toll. How could they ask their families to face a Winter under such hardships?

Joe and Jack counted themselves lucky; at least they had jobs to go back to. Longer hours meant the owners could cut their costs by reducing their work force. Those who had been most outspoken during the strike, now found themselves blacklisted, wiped off the payroll, thrown out of their colliery houses. Both knew families who had been driven out to live in sheds on their allotments; some, faced with no alternative, were living in the caves in the cliffs that lined the beaches.

Kicking their muddy boots off at the back door, the men were glad to get into the relative warmth of the kitchen. Ellen and Eva were playing with the babies in front of the fire. The women were well wrapped up, wearing thick knitted cardigans over woollen dresses. Hearing the men come in, Ellen threw a couple of pieces of wood onto the fire and shifted the kettle further over the flames to boil.

"Have you fetched anything for the pot, Jack?" Ellen enquired hopefully.

"Just a few leeks and parsnips," Jack replied. "Oh, and we necked one of the hens too. She might be a bit stringy mind, she's that old but I'm sure you'll work wonders as usual, pet." He bent down to scoop up Freddy, who was babbling away at him with his arms raised expectantly above his head. He threw the baby up and down in the air, to Freddy's obvious delight.

"We bumped into Stan Barlow up the road. He sez

there's to be a meeting at the Welfare tomorrow; the owners and the Union have reached an agreement."

Eva wished Joe looked a bit more optimistic about this news. "Maybe it won't be that bad, Joe; at least they've managed to agree on something at last." Standing up, she continued. "Here, you take our Tommy while Ellen and I sort out the dinner. We'll eat up here; it's easier keeping one fire going as two."

The two women retired into the scullery to pluck and prepare the hen ready for the pot. That and the vegetables would make a fine stew. As they worked they speculated on what the immediate future might hold. "At least we should have a couple of pays before Christmas," Ellen said, "but it's still going to be a sorry one."

"Yes," Eva agreed, "But not as sorry as those who've lost everything. I was wondering, Ellen, couldn't the women get together and try to do something for those who've been turned out of their homes. I can't imagine how they are managing and some of them have four or five children, too."

"Aye, I'm afraid it's the women and kids who pay the price for their husband's actions as usual. Maybe the men would have thought twice about being so militant if they knew they'd be out on the street once the strike ended." Ellen continued plucking, carefully depositing the soft feathers into the now empty sack; they would do to stuff a cushion later.

"Jean was saying the church is managing to run a soup kitchen for the worst off. Some of the more well-off parishes are still sending in donations of food and old clothes." Eva was peeling and chopping the parsnips, "I was thinking, once we get a pay, maybe some of us could get together, like we used to, and bake a few pies and some bread to give them. Do you think the others would be willing, Ellen?"

"Some will, Eva but then there's always some who have very short memories. We can but ask. Now let's get this pan onto the fire or we'll be eating this stew at bed-time."

When Joe returned from the union meeting on Sunday, Eva could see the disappointment on his face. As they had thought, the men would be paid less for working longer hours. "That means they'll need less men to get the coal out," Joe informed her, "and those still workin' will have to manage on less money. All those months of doing without for nowt!"

Eva couldn't blame him for feeling angry; once again the miners' grievances seemed to have fallen on deaf ears. They were no further forward in their fight for fair pay. She guided her husband to his seat by the fire and placed a comforting hand on his shoulder.

"They say we'll have to agree to all muck in and work together when needed, as if we don't already do that, and there's to be no sitting at the kist, like we're a load of shirkers."

"Was there nothing good come out of it at all, Joe?" Eva said trying to find some way to dissipate his anger.

"Well, there's to be a District Board set up to sort out any future disputes. It's to be run by an independent Chairman so's both sides'll get a fair hearing. And they're deeing away with piecework so everyone gets the same rate no matter what face they're working.

"Those datal men on the lowest wage are to get their basic week made up to 6s 8½d, what they call the subsistence, so that's good I suppose. And it actually says no man will be victimised 'cos of what they did in the dispute. 'Course that's rubbish 'cos they'll need less men to do the same jobs with longer hours so they'll not set anyone back on they've already blacklisted."

Eva felt so sad for her husband and the thousands like him who had fought unsuccessfully for their rights. She only hoped this new District Board would not simply be another puppet for the owners. "Never mind pet, you all did your best; at least you didn't all roll over like the railwaymen did. Let's hope we can all get back to normal now."

"There'll still be those who want to hold out for a National Agreement rather than these separate District ones, but I think they'll get little support from the men. We just haven't the heart anymore.

"Anyway, enough of this," Joe rose and took Eva into his arms. "One more bit of good news: they're gonna lead the coals this week, as soon as we've gone back, so at least we'll be able to keep warm."

"That's great, Joe. The first thing I'll do is have a lovely long soak in a hot bath in front of a roaring fire."

With a glint in his eye, Joe countered, "Do you think there'll be enough room in that old tin bath for two, pet?"

CHAPTER THIRTY-EIGHT

Rising at six, Joe raked the fire back into life, before settling the kettle on the coals to boil. Seconds later, Eva joined him in the kitchen. "Sorry, pet, I didn't hear the alarm go off. I'll soon have your breakfast sorted."

"I knocked the alarm off before it rang; I didn't want to wake you. I'm quite capable of seein' to me own breakfast, you know." He'd also wanted a few minutes alone to sort out his feelings; part of him wasn't looking forward to going back down into that black hole but another part of him said it would be good to be working again, earning the money to keep his family.

Eva was affronted, "Since when have I ever lain abed while you went off to work?" She busied herself frying up a couple of eggs for him. There would be no bacon until they got a pay but the eggs should keep him going until bait time. "What do you want for your bait?" she asked automatically.

Amused, Joe replied, "Oh I'll have some nice roast beef smothered in horse radish sauce, if you please."

Eva looked up sharply then laughed at herself, "I reckon you'll have to make do with jam'n'bread this week, if that's alright m'lord?"

Joe seated himself at the table, while she dished up the food onto his plate and cut two slices of bread from the loaf. She stationed herself at the opposite side of the table and studied him as she readied his bait. "How's it feel to be going back?"

She was quite relieved when he responded, "It feels good, lass. It'll be great to be back among the lads and doin' a fair day's work. Although, if things are as bad down there as some of the deputies say, I might have a different view by the time I come home."

Eva smiled brightly, "Oh you know what those deputies are like. One thing sure to put them off is the thought of hard work."

"True," Joe said, "and we'll have to hear all about how there wouldn't be any pit to go back to if they hadn't held it together these last months." A cloud crossed over Joe's face as his thoughts went back to Ned Sherringham; he'd never make deputy now, would he? "Right I'll just go and give Tommy a kiss then I'd better get goin' wouldn't do to be late my first shift back."

All across the village, men were emerging into the

freezing blackness, pulling coats tighter against the biting North wind. In their kitchens, women listened to their heavy feet as they pounded the cobbles on their way to work. Relief poured through the whole community as normality was being restored.

Men teemed through the pit gates and across the yard to collect their tokens and lamps before packing themselves tightly into the cages to descend into the inky depths below. Their voices rose and fell as they greeted friends and swapped stories about the strike. Some could be heard above the rest, vilifying scabs and the government who had betrayed them but generally the atmosphere was a convivial one.

At the pit head, Joe sought out Stan in the crowd, greeting him warmly with a friendly slap on the back. "Now marra, how's it goin'?"

"It's good to be back, lad. You ready for a hard shift then?" Just then they heard a shout from behind them. It was Fred; the three musketeers were back in action.

Dropping like a stone through the blackness, Joe welcomed the familiar lurch in his stomach and the whistle of the air rushing past. A hush had descended over the men packed tightly into the cages; it was almost as if they were holding their breaths.

Spilling out into the shaft bottom, they separated into their teams, each heading off towards their designated face. There were signs of neglect all around them. A mine is like a living thing; left to its own devices it continues to shift and settle, challenging the weak efforts of man to contain it. In the blackness they were surrounded by sounds of wooden props cracking and sinking under the strain of supporting hundreds of feet of stone and coal above them.

It was a long walk into the face. Here and there the roof had fallen, scattering stone across the tunnels, making progress difficult. Leaving some men behind to get on with the job of clearing the way, Joe and the rest of the men pushed on to the coal face. At least, so far, most of the props and girders still held. They kept a close eye on their lamps; the deputies would have regularly checked for any gas build-ups, but you could never be too careful.

Luckily, there seemed to have been little damage to the iron rails, and the ponies could bring in tubs carrying new props and girders and pull out those filled with stone to be emptied on the surface. Joe, Stan and Fred constantly checked the condition of the roof as they progressed. In some places they had to halt the men while they brought down unsafe material then re-instate the metal roof girders.

Bert appeared half-way into the shift and told them to stop for their bait. Mindful of the danger, each man sought a sturdy prop to hang his lamp on and rest his back against. They ate greedily, gratefully swigging water from their bottles. Months of relative inactivity had weakened backs and legs and they would all feel the after effects of their labours.

By the end of the shift they had made it half-way to the face; the next shift would pick up where they left off. Dragging their feet wearily they set off on the long walk back to the shaft bottom to catch the cages up to bank. They are ghosts, Joe thought, their faces white not black, covered in stone dust instead of coal. Everyone silent, too tired to talk.

The women in their kitchens heard the boots against the cobbles; waited apprehensively for the men to come back from the pit. Baths half-filled with hot water, ready to receive their aching bodies. Make do and mend meals, mostly vegetables and a little meat, ticked on 'til payday from the local butcher, simmered in pots and pans in ovens or on fires. Waiting for the workers return.

Returning the next day, at last the ways were clear as far as to most coal faces but it would be a much more difficult task to get them working again. There was nothing for it but to apply brute force to recover the coal cutting machines. First they had to dig out the shattered wooden props, crushed by the sinking roof, replacing them with strong new ones. Foot by foot the face was secured, and the machinery uncovered. It took all week, but at last some faces were ready to go back into production.

CHAPTER THIRTY-NINE

Christmas and New Year came and went. There was little to go round; most people were still trying to clear off the debts they had accrued during the dispute. Even Thomas Greenall was finding it difficult; who knew how long he would have to wait for his customers to clear their accounts. To give him his due, he never queried for one moment that every debt would be paid; miners were exceedingly hard working and honest.

Joe, Eva and little Tommy had spent Christmas with her parents in Wain Hill. Eva had to admit it was nice to feel rather spoiled for once, enjoying the more opulent surroundings of her childhood home. Joe took the opportunity to look up some of his old mates and Ginny was delighted to be able to spend some time getting to know her youngest nephew better.

On Christmas Eve they all attended Midnight Mass and Christmas Day saw everyone, including Ginny and her friend Jimmy Bell, who seemed to be a more or less permanent fixture in her life now, sitting around the dinner table in Tom and Bella's dining room. Everyone wore the colourful, paper party hats gleaned from the Christmas crackers and there was much jollity and laughter.

Later, sitting in front of her old dressing table mirror, Eva regarded her reflection pensively. Where was that naive young girl who had been so excited getting ready for her first dance? She was not surprised when she heard the door open behind her and her mother entered the room.

"Everything alright, dear?" Bella enquired, walking up to stand behind Eva, placing her hands gently on her shoulders.

Eva turned on her stool to face her. "Everything's fine Mam. I was just making the most of a little peace and quiet, that's all." She studied her mother's face. There were a few more wrinkles and one or two streaks of silver in her hair.

"So, there's nothing you want to tell me then?" Bella wheedled.

Eva laughed, "No Mam, and I'm definitely not pregnant so you can get that idea out of your head. Joe and I have both agreed that we'll need to be a lot more secure money wise before we think about a brother or sister for Tommy."

Bella looked a little crest-fallen, another baby would have been nice. "I'm sure I don't know what you mean," she protested rather weakly, "and I think that's perfectly sensible of you, dear. Although, you know, mistakes do happen."

Eva jumped up and hugged her mother tightly, "And when they do, you'll be the first to know, I promise." Linking her mother's arm, she guided her back out of the room and down the stairs to join the others in the living room from where they could already hear much laughter.

It was a delight to find her father, down on all fours on the carpet, with Tommy seated firmly on his back, singing 'Horsey, horsey don't you stop!'' although his galloping was more of a clumsy plod. If only his business friends could see him now!

Although they had all enjoyed Christmas, Eva was quite relieved to head home on the day after Boxing Day; she had missed Ellen, Jack and their children and was eager to get back to normality. Eva and Joe spent New Year quietly, at home, although Joe still joined the other husbands in the street to await the pit hooter announcing midnight before being admitted as first foot. He threw his coal onto the fire, accepted his glass and raised it to welcome in the New Year. "Let's hope this year is better than the last!"

Taking Eva into his arms, he kissed her deeply. "I love you, Mrs. Fishburn," he proclaimed, his voice choked with emotion.

Eva gazed lovingly into his eyes, "Show me!"

CHAPTER FORTY

Having tasted the rewards of life outside the everyday routine of cooking, cleaning and shopping, many women could have found it difficult to slip back into their old pre-strike roles. And, although the strike was ended there were still hard times ahead for many families.

Those who had been black-listed by the coal owners, found it almost impossible to secure work and many families were living in abject poverty in the poorest of housing, in sheds, in caves or even enduring the Winter in tents. Some had moved away to seek work in the towns and cities.

Eva, Ellen and Jean continued to work in the Church soup kitchen, although they found it more difficult to secure enough donations especially in the way of fresh vegetables. Luckily, a local farmer at Holm Hill, who had done his best to support the miners during the strike, was willing to help the needy now. He opened up one of his clamps of potatoes and also gave some of the turnips he had laid by to feed his animals over the winter; these with the addition of a few winter cabbages and some freshly made stotties, would make a nourishing, if not tasty, stew.

Eva silently thanked her parents for the sturdy pram they had bought for Tommy, as she pushed it up the hill towards the Church Hall. Laden down as it was with foodstuffs donated by friends and neighbours, it took all her strength to keep it moving up the steep main street.

It was a miserable Wednesday morning; the piercing wind, blowing straight off the pitiless North Sea, beat the freezing rain mercilessly against her bent back. Her thick woollen coat was already half sodden and water ran freely down over her face from the brim of her hat. Safely tucked in under his pram blankets, the raised hood and rain cover keeping out the filthy weather, Tommy slept on oblivious.

Ellen called to her from across the street, as she came out of the butchers. "Eva, hold on!" She hurried over the road to join her sister-in-law, clutching a brown shopping bag in both hands. "Harry's just given me a load of bones and by the looks of them there's still be plenty meat left on. That'll help put some flavour into the stew."

"That's great Ellen. It's wonderful how many people find it in their hearts to help those less fortunate than themselves." Eva smiled.

"Yeah, but there's some as seem to have a short memory when it comes to remembering what it's like to have an empty belly. I called at Daisy Bradshaw's this morning to see if she had owt to give and she sent me off with a flea in my ear. She even had the cheek to start quoting Scripture at me. 'Those louts'll get nothing off me: 'Ye shall reap as ye shall sow' she says. I felt like saying she should listen to herself but I know better than to stand and argue with the likes of her on the doorstep for all to hear."

Eva thought it was a brave woman who would take on her sister-in-law when she had her dander up. "Never mind Ellen, there are still enough of us who do care. We can do without the likes of Daisy, thank goodness."

Entering the Church Hall, they paused in the lobby to remove their wet things, shaking off the worst of the rain and hanging their coats on the hooks on the far wall. They could tell by the voices coming from the larger hall that some of the other women were already there. Eva pushed the pram into the room and started unloading the contents from beneath it.

Betty Soulsby hurried across to help her. "Oh, I'm pleased to see you've brought more flour, lass, we're runnin' a bit low. We'll get the dough mixed and set to prove before we start on the veg." it was obvious Betty considered herself to be the manager but to be fair the rest of the women were more than willing to let her take control of the kitchen. It wasn't as if she didn't also do more than her fair share of the work too. Eva thought Betty was trying to make up for the fact that as a deputy, Bert, her husband, had not been out on strike with the rest of the men. It seemed she was determined to show that she cared just as much about her community as the rest of the women.

Once the bread was kneaded, they all set about peeling and chopping; while potatoes and swedes would make up the bulk of stew, there were also onions and kale and of course the beef bones. Everything was tossed into a huge iron cauldron set atop a gas ring. A broom shank had been cut in two and was used to stir the contents regularly to stop it from catching.

Eva's ears pricked up as she caught the gist of the conversation going on between Betty and Martha Tinsdale about women joining the Labour Party. "But can women still join if they don't have a job? I mean it is a 'labour' party isn't it?"

"That just means that they stand for the working man Betty not the bosses and privileged classes. I went to listen to a talk by Margaret Bondfield; she said more women should join the Labour Party if they wanted to have a say in how the country should be run."

As Eva said to Ellen later, it had certainly given her food for thought; the strike could never have lasted so long but for the support of the women encouraging and sustaining their menfolk. Didn't they deserve some say in their future.

The local Labour council continued to provide free school meals to those children whose parents had no visible means of support and the Miners' Federation contributed food vouchers to the neediest. Many miners managed to donate a few coppers from their reduced wages or gave up some of their coal allowance to support those they had once laboured beside; they would not desert their friends and neighbours now in their hour of need. The coal owners might not like this state of affairs but there was little they could do about it without inciting a fierce reaction from their workforce.

Joe became an avid reader of the national newspapers which increasingly seemed to side with the working classes. In fact, the Conservative Government and the owners may have won the battle against the miners in the short term but the war was far from over. Despite doing their best to label the miners as revolutionaries, the public were not so easily deceived. Many deplored the way the miners had been treated and the terrible conditions in which they had to work.

Public opinion turned against the Conservatives; many felt they could not be trusted. In the next three years the Tories lost every bi-election and subsequently in 1929, the General Election. Labour backed by the Liberals formed the new government. Following the Wall Street Crash, many more suffered during the Depression, but the Mining Communities were in a stronger position than most to weather the storm. In 1930 there was much rejoicing in the Colliery Club when the news came through that The Coal Mine Act had been passed; this

helped to fix reasonable coal prices and wages, the shifts were set back to seven and a half hours and there were promises of a national agreement and proposed improvements in conditions and safety down the mines. It seemed the strike had been effective after all.

Over the next few years Eva and Ellen each had several more children and their houses were always filled with much laughter. Their busy lives did not deter them from joining the local Labour Party with their husbands. They could see that a better future for miners lay in finding a political rather than an activist solution to their problems.

No-one could have foreseen the even greater threat to come.

ABOUT THE AUTHOR

Ethel Stirman lives on the East coast of Durham and comes from a mining family. She is a member of local writing groups and has successfully written several short stories and poems. 'Not a Minute on the Day' is her first novel.

Made in the USA
Columbia, SC
27 February 2018